A Case of Missing on Midthorpe
A Midthorpe Murder Mystery (#1)

David W Robinson

www.darkstroke.com

Copyright © 2019 by David W Robinson
Cover Photography by Adobe Stock © aanbetta
Design by soqoqo
All rights reserved.

No part of this book may be used or reproduced in any manner whatsoever without written permission of the author or Crooked Cat Books except for brief quotations used for promotion or in reviews. This is a work of fiction. Names, characters, and incidents are used fictitiously.

First Dark Edition, darkstroke. 2019

Discover us online:
www.darkstroke.com

Find us on instagram:
www.instagram.com/darkstrokebooks

Include **#darkstroke** in a photo of yourself holding his book on Instagram and **something nice will happen.**

About the Author

David Robinson is a Yorkshireman now living in Manchester. Driven by a huge, cynical sense of humour, he's been a writer for over thirty years having begun with magazine articles before moving on to novels and TV scripts.

He has little to do with his life other than write, as a consequence of which his output is prodigious. Thankfully most of it is never seen by the great reading public of the world.

He has worked closely with Crooked Cat Books and darkstroke since 2012, when The Filey Connection, the very first Sanford 3rd Age Club Mystery, was published.

Describing himself as the Doyen of Domestic Disasters he can be found blogging at **www.dwrob.com** and he appears frequently on video (written, produced and starring himself) dispensing his mocking humour at **www.youtube.com/user/ Dwrob96/videos**

The Midthorpe Murder Mystery series:
A Case of Missing on Midthorpe
A Case of Bloodshed in Benidorm

The STAC Mystery series:
The Filey Connection
The I-Spy Murders
A Halloween Homicide
A Murder for Christmas
Murder at the Murder Mystery Weekend
My Deadly Valentine
The Chocolate Egg Murders
The Summer Wedding Murder
Costa del Murder
Christmas Crackers
Death in Distribution
A Killing in the Family
A Theatrical Murder
Trial by Fire
Peril in Palmanova
The Squire's Lodge Murders
Murder at the Treasure Hunt
A Cornish Killing

A Case of Missing on Midthorpe

A Midthorpe Murder Mystery (#1)

Chapter One

"Careful… I mean it, Nate. This thing's loaded."

Nathan Perry's eyes narrowed to tiny points of malevolence. "I'm sick of you and your toffees. This punter wants his money back or the real thing, and if you don't pay up, I'll make sure he comes looking for you."

"You'll keep your mouth shut. You're in this just as deeply as the rest of us. And if he wants his money back, that's your pigeon, not mine. What the hell were you doing selling to a man like him in the first place?"

"Making money for you, that's what."

"And you didn't get your share? No, forget it, Nate. You got yourself into this mess, you get yourself out of it."

Nathan moved forward, the twin barrels of the Webley twelve gauge confronted him again. He grabbed the barrel.

"Don't you threaten me."

He dragged the gun towards him. Both barrels exploded into his chest, and he fell back to the cold, concrete floor.

"Damn. Damn and blast you, you bloody idiot." Panic gripped him temporarily, and he had to force himself to calm down, taking deep breaths, letting them out slowly, evenly. He'd been in this position before, and it was not intractable.

He replaced the shotgun in the locker, then stepped outside, looking up and down the rough lane. No one to be seen. It was hardly surprising. At this time on a bitterly cold January evening, most people were at home sitting in front of the box.

He reversed his car up to the shutter, opened the boot, then went back into the small workshop. Digging out a set of overalls, he put them on, raised the shutter and, his stomach heaving, limbs trembling, manhandled the dead youth into the car boot, slammed the lid down, and locked it.

Then he lowered and secured the shutter, before setting about cleaning up the mess of blood on the concrete floor. It was hard work, but fortunately, the nature of his operation meant he had plenty of serious cleaning fluids available.

Half an hour later the job was done. All that remained now was to get rid of the rest of the evidence: Nate Perry.

From the back of the workshop, he took out a shovel, and stripped off his overalls. They were covered in blood, too. They would have to be burned. He couldn't leave them lying around here. His operation was (in his opinion) not really illegal, but he couldn't risk the filth turning up and finding a set of bloodstained working clothes. By the same token, he couldn't dump them with Nate's body, just in case someone found the lad, and the forensic scientists employed by the police, linked them to him.

Throwing a shovel and the overalls into the boot, he locked up the workshop, and climbed behind the wheel. There was only one place to get rid of the boy. It would be hard work, and he'd be lucky if he got to bed this side of two in the morning.

"Might have to chuck a sickie tomorrow," he said to himself as he started the engine and drove away.

***

Aside from a dim glow penetrating the thick, blood red curtains, the house appeared to be in total darkness. They looked around the well-kept front garden, and up the paved drive to the side of the house. There was no one, and nothing to be seen. The biting cold of a January night kept the occupants and their neighbours indoors.

Dressed from head to toe in dark clothing, they pulled balaclava masks down, covering their faces. Their hands were shrouded in woolly gloves, keeping out the cold, keeping out the fingerprints. Caution was the watchword. Neither of them had ever been in serious trouble with the police, and now was not the time to start.

"You ready, man?" The first man's voice was not much

above a whisper.

The other held up the wheelbrace and scissor-jack. "You got the props?"

The first held up three house bricks. "Go for it."

They crept up the drive, crouching low, taking advantage of the hedgerows to keep them even deeper in the shadows.

"What if he's got one of them automatic lights at the door?"

"Well, we're not gonna knock on the door, are we?"

"Yeah, but, they have a wide field."

Behind his mask, the second man's eyes screwed up into a puzzled stare. "We're not in a field, you numpty. This is his drive. That's why it's got the car parked in it."

The first man clucked impatiently. "I keep forgetting I'm working with a banana. Any hassle, and we leg it. Right? Drop everything and run for it."

The second man held up the jack and wheelbrace. "These are my dad's. No way am I leaving these behind."

They continued their slow ascent up the steep drive, crouching even lower as they neared the black BMW, keeping to the offside, away from the house wall and the danger of motion-sensitive security lights.

Gently sliding the jack under the car, the second man chortled with glee. "Alloys. No badge. Bloke like him, an'all. I thought they was supposed to be all for the poor."

The first man fiddled with the wheelbrace, attaching it to the nuts. "Yeah? Since when did he drop you a coupla bob? They're all the same, man. Get it jacked up."

His partner began to turn the screw at the end of the jack. It gave a tiny squeak, and they paused, freezing, looking around, expecting someone, anyone, coming to investigate the noise. When nothing happened, he turned the jack again.

The door of the house opened, the far side of the car was flooded with light, and they froze again. Whoever was there could not see them, but every muscle in their bodies was tense, ready to run for it.

His voice, a cultured, educated English accent, reached them. "Go on. Go and have a wee. That's a good girl."

They heard the door close again and breathed a silent sigh of relief.

The first man was struggling to fit the wheelbrace onto the nuts. "Vicious bastard. Don't tell me they're locking nuts."

His pal turned the scissor jack again. "You can do it."

From behind came a strange, panting sound. The wheelbrace operator turned his head and stared into the dark, evil eyes of the hound from hell. She probably weighed more than the pair of them put together. Saliva dripped from the slobbering lips, the eyes were narrowed on their target, which as far as the first man was concerned, was his backside.

Without warning, she gave a bark loud enough to be heard three streets away.

With cries of terror, they stood up and ran for it, and while the first man dropped his bricks and the wheelbrace, the second had enough sense permeating his dread, to collect his father's jack and that same wheelbrace before hurrying after his partner.

The Rottweiler bounded after them, her stumpy tail wagging from side to side, her bark reaching their ears, and spurring them to greater speed.

They dashed across the road, leapt over the low wall into Midthorpe Park, and scuttled away into the small clutch of trees just inside the boundary wall. Pausing, looking back, they could see the giant dog, her paws resting on the wall, barking after them.

Back at the house, the door opened, and a security light came on once again. The householder raised his voice. "Sue. Come on, Sue. That's enough of that. Come on. Good girl."

Responding to her master's voice, the dog turned and padded back across the road.

"You dummy. I thought you'd cased the place. How come you didn't know they had a bleeding lion for a pet?"

The second raised his balaclava, and ran a shaking hand across his forehead. "I checked the car, not the bod what owns it. Did you get rid of the bricks?"

"Do fish crap in the sea? Anyway, you should know, you nearly fell over them." The first man pulled back his sleeve and checked his watch. "Ten o'clock. Anywhere else you can think of?"

"Not with alloys. Suppose we could do a couple of regular wheels."

"Yeah, and end up with half the dosh we should have."

"It's called cutting your losses. Better with a tenner each than nothing at all." He sighed. "You got any toffees?"

His partner ferreted through his pockets and came out with a single pill smothered in cheap bubblewrap. "One Fiagara. You on a promise or something?"

"Since when do I need help getting it up?" The other tutted. "I was thinking of hitting the Midden and selling a few."

"Well, we could make a fiver with this."

"Forget it. I'm going home, taking me dad's tackle back."

Removing the masks, they trudged back towards the main entrance, and as they passed through the stone pillars, the beam of headlights coming from the road opposite, the one that led back to the estate, picked them out.

The car came straight down the hill, paused at the main road, and drove across, stopping in the park gates.

The window came down. "All right, lads? Up to your usual tricks?"

"Looking for a bit of action, that's all," the first man said. "You got any gear?"

The driver laughed. "Not tonight. On a promise down there." He nodded into the park. "I'll catch you both later." He put the car in gear, and drove off, leaving them staring enviously after him.

***

Everyone knew that the gardeners' compound in Midthorpe Park was about as secure as a frayed washing line in a hurricane.

True, there was a padlock on the gate, but a pair of bolt cutters would soon take care of it. The trouble was, he had no bolt cutters. Instead, he employed a couple of bricks as a makeshift hammer and anvil, and after a few hefty cracks, the lock snapped away. Tossing the bricks to one side, he made his way into the compound, collected a wheelbarrow, and retraced his steps, pushing the gate closed behind him, before ambling off to his car, 200 yards away.

Once there, he cast a final check round to ensure there was no one watching him. Even at this time of year, Midthorpe Park had a reputation as the ideal spot for a bit of extramarital, horizontal PT.

Satisfied that he was totally alone, he opened the boot, put on the overalls, and rolled Nate's body into the barrow. Dropping the shovel in on top of the body, he closed the boot, switched on his flashlight, and with it held awkwardly in one hand, made his way into Midthorpe Woods.

It was a bit unfortunate bumping into those two clowns at the park gates. When news of Nate's disappearance spread, they would ask awkward questions. As luck would have it, neither of them was blessed with any great intelligence, and they would be easy to shut up. They worked for him just as Nate had done, and he knew enough about their trade in stolen wheels to keep them quiet.

Thinking about it as he made his way along the pitch dark path through the woods, there would be no need for them to know that Nate was dead. This was Midthorpe; one of the worst council estates in Leeds. Its reputation meant the police considered it a no-go area, and young people regularly disappeared from this part of the city, most of them making for London, Blackpool in Scarborough, or even Bradford... Anywhere but Midthorpe.

He reached his destination, a small hollow deep in the woods. Letting the wheelbarrow stand, he began to dig.

Circumstances favoured him once more. The winter had been wet rather than icy, and the ground was soft, yielding. Even so, it was hard work digging out a hole large enough to accommodate a body, and then shovelling earth back in, and finally topping it off with a layer of dead vegetation.

Bathed in sweat, he dropped the shovel in the empty wheelbarrow and began to make his way back to his car.

As he reached the end of the path, close to the car park, he killed his flashlight. Security! Bugger. He'd forgotten about them.

With the same caution as utilised by the police, there were two of them, and they were checking his car. He waited, hidden in the darkness. They would soon be gone.

"Tougher man than I am," he heard one of them say. "I meanersay, it's one thing getting your legover in this kinda weather, but you should be on the back seat of the car, not in the woods."

"It could be nicked. Are we gonna log it?"

"Nah. The boss'll only wanna know why we didn't follow it up with Swansea to find out who owns it. Let's leave it this time, and if it's still here on the next round, then we'll log it."

Listening to them, he buried the silent sigh of relief. Who said there were no advantages to the general laziness of Midthorpers?

He watched them drive off, gave it another few minutes, then stepped out of the inky blackness, hurried to his car, dropped the shovel into the boot, and finally returned the wheelbarrow to the gardeners' compound, leaving it exactly as he found it, propped up against a stack of compost bags.

Returning to the car, he removed the overalls, and dropped them in the boot, and as a final check shone his torch around the interior of the boot. There were traces of what looked like blood here and there. Another item to add to his checklist. The interior of the car would need a thorough scrubbing with cleaning fluid and disinfectant.

Five minutes later, he drove out of the park and back to his workshop. Further down the rough lane was a skip outside a pallet yard. They used it for dumping broken pallets, and it caught fire (deliberately) so often that he was forced to wonder why the contractor who owned the skip was prepared to go on leaving it there.

Such questions were irrelevant to him. Siphoning a half litre of petrol from his car, he dropped the overalls in the skip, soaked them in unleaded, and then dug out a cigarette lighter. He was tempted to light a cigarette first, but he realised that he stank of petrol. His intention was to burn the overalls, not himself. Subduing his nicotine craving, he rolled a sheet of newspaper into a tight knot, lit it, and dropped it on the overalls.

With a WHOOSH, flames leapt into the dark, winter sky, and he was forced to back off. Indeed, the speed at which the fire took hold, compelled him to leap back into his car, turn round and get the hell out of there before half the lane went up in smoke.

As he reached the main road at the top, turning right and then left into Midthorpe estate, the glow of his hastily conceived efforts at disposing of evidence could be seen in the rearview mirror. Making a mental note that he still had to attend to the shovel and the boot of his car, he turned into the street where he lived, and reversed sedately into his drive.

Aside from the unexpected ferocity of the conflagration in the skip (he would later learn that the owner of the pallet yard had planned to torch the skip the following night, and the wood was already soaked in various fuel oils) it had been a successful evening's work.

Chapter Two

Raymond Baldock placed a tube of mints and a small bottle of water on the counter. "I'd like two first class stamps, please."

Ivan Haigh reached below the counter, into a drawer, came out with a book of first class stamps, from which he tore off two, and placed them on the counter with the other items. He then took a pencil from his ear, snatched a notebook and scribbled down the prices.

"Mints, sixty-five pee, water, seventy-nine pee, one first class stamp, sixty-seven pee, one first class stamp, sixty-seven pee. Right, chief, all up, that's…" He ran through them with his pencil, adding up the numbers. "Two pounds seventy-seven, for cash." He held out his hand.

"Two pounds seventy eight," Baldock insisted.

"What?"

"You have four odd numbers. It's impossible for them to come to an odd number. They must come to an even number, two sevens are fourteen, nine plus five also makes fourteen, two fourteens are twenty-eight, so the final price must end in eight." Baldock became distantly aware of a woman customer queuing behind him and concluded his impromptu lecture. "Assuming the remainder of your arithmetic is correct, it must come to two pounds seventy eight, not seventy-seven."

Haigh appeared slightly fazed. "What are you? Some kind of mathematician?"

"No. It's just that when I went to school, instead of secretly skimming through the latest Star Wars comic during arithmetic lessons, I listened and learned."

Haigh gazed suspiciously upon Baldock as if suspecting a

brazen effort to belittle and defraud him in front of his customers. Taking a half pace to his left, he punched the numbers into the cash register, which gave the answer £2.78 in glowing, green LED characters.

"All right. Two pounds and seventy-*eight* pee."

Baldock blinked rapidly. "You have a till which can add up the numbers, why didn't you use it?"

With a broad grin, Haigh tapped his temple. "Brain training, boss. Gotta keep the old mind active. If you don't use it, you lose it."

"I see. Well, you obviously have some way to go yet, so keep it up." Baldock reached into his wallet, pulled out a debit card and placed it on the counter.

Haigh stared from the card, up at Baldock, back to the card, and back to Baldock. "Cash," he insisted.

"I don't have any cash on me."

"Do you know how much profit I make on those bits?" Haigh gestured broadly at the items on the counter. "Not enough to cover what the bank'll charge me for taking your card. Cash only." He held out his hand.

A sigh came from the irritated woman behind Baldock. Ignoring her, he concentrated on the young shopkeeper. "Do you know who I am?"

"Nope."

"I'm Raymond Baldock. The novelist."

Haigh shrugged, his face a blank. "So what do you want? An Oscar?"

"I created the Richard Headingley series."

Haigh appeared as dumfounded as ever. "This gets better. Lemme tell you summat, pal. The only Richard Heads I meet are usually the other side of the counter from me."

"Headingley, not Head. Do you read books?"

"Nope."

"But you can actually read?"

"Acourse I can bloody read. I'm not illegible."

"Merely illiterate." Leaning forward, Baldock loomed over the smaller shopkeeper. "I am *the* Raymond Baldock. I'm the most successful man ever to come from Midthorpe.

My last novel sold over three hundred thousand copies in less than six months, and it's already been transcribed for television. I'm worth more than the stock held in this entire parade of shops and I do not carry cash."

More sighs from the woman behind, and Haigh shrugged as he gathered back the four items on the counter. "No cash, no stamps, mints or water."

Baldock's eyebrows shot up. Once more he sensed the impatience of the woman behind him and forced himself to concentrate on the determined minion behind the counter. "I need the stamps. They're the reason I came in here." He held up two white envelopes, both addressed in his flowing handwriting, both devoid of stamps.

Haigh deployed his pencil as a pointer and aimed it through the windows. "There's a hole in wall on the other side of the road. It's outside the bank, which I suppose you own. Go there, draw some cash, or go somewhere else for your stamps. If you can find anywhere else where they'll take plastic."

"Now listen—"

"Acourse, if you want to wander round my shop, buy a few more things, get the bill to something over a tenner, I'll take your card."

"That's tantamount to blackmail."

"I'm not tanting, I'm just saying—"

"Oh, for God's sake…" Finally losing her cool, the woman from behind pushed past Baldock. "Here, Ivan. Three pounds. Give me his bloody change and get a move on."

"Right on, Lisa." Haigh took the money, pushed the trivial goods across to Baldock, who took them graciously, before backing off. "You'll find the post box in—"

This time, it was Baldock who interrupted Haigh. "I know where the post box is. I grew up round here." With a bleak, half smile of thanks aimed at the woman, he marched out of the shop.

Once out on the broad pavements of Midthorpe Avenue, while attaching the stamps to the envelopes, he quickly learned that he no longer knew where the post box was.

Shops lined either side of the road, from the fish 'n' chip shop and newsagents opposite, to Haighs minimarket and the Midthorpe Uni-Stylist on this side. When he was a boy, the hair stylist had been a greengrocer and Haighs (run by the elder Mr Haigh) had been a sub-post office, outside which stood the required mailbox.

It was no longer there and worse, he could not see it anywhere.

Across the road, further on from the newsagents was the bank, where it had always been, flanked by a tanning salon and another takeaway. On this side, was a bakery, a branch of a national chain of bookmakers, and a butchers, beyond which was a small branch of a national supermarket. After parking his Mercedes, Raymond had been tempted to go in there, but when he glanced through the windows he saw Amanda Armitage filling shelves. He had recognised her, and he was certain she would recognise him. He did not want to be recognised, hence his brisk walk down to Haighs, where, curiously enough, it might have been more helpful if Haigh the younger *had* recognised him.

As matters stood, he owed a complete stranger almost three pounds, he couldn't find the post box and he had no wish to chew on the humble pie required to go back into Haigh's and ask.

Standing on the pavement, bathed in July sunshine, he caught sight of his reflection in the hairdresser's window, and even to himself, he looked like a little boy lost. Correction, a little boy lost with a woman bearing down on him. His peripheral vision registered her shadow moving across the pavement and he turned to meet the woman who had come to his rescue.

Brown eyes under a dark fringe of hair, narrowed on him, her lips, tightly drawn, were ready to give him a piece of her mind, and as she approached, Baldock rehearsed his opening line, but it was with the feeling that she was not a complete stranger. He was sure he knew her.

"I, er… thank you for helping in there. I owe you three pounds."

"Two pounds seventy-eight." A stern, disapproving reminder.

There was something about those tight lips. Or was it the snug fit of her skirt and the delightful curvature beneath her shining white business shirt, both accentuating a body which was well looked-after. He frowned internally. He valued intellect over the physical, and there was a clarity in those eyes which spoke of someone above the Midthorpe average. Did he know her or was he imagining it?

"We won't quibble over twenty-two pence. If you could give me a few minutes, I'll go over to the bank and draw some cash."

"I don't have a few minutes. I'm late as it is. Largely thanks to you arguing with Ivan. You can catch me at the Health Centre. Counselling."

He smiled knowingly. "Midthorpe did that to a lot of people."

The brow furrowed, the lips drew tighter. "What?"

"Put them into counselling. As I said, I grew up here and —"

"I am the counsellor." She interrupted. "Young Ivan may not recognise you, but I'll bet his father would, and I certainly do."

"Ah… Oh… You have me at a disadvantage. I feel I should know you too, but I can't quite place you."

"Lisa Yeoman."

Memories flooded his mind. "Right. Excellent. Of course I know you. We were the only two Midthorpers to make it to university."

"From our year," Lisa added. "You were a proper pain in the bottom then, Raymond. It's nice to see that your fame and fortune haven't changed you one bit. If you wanted to use a debit card, why didn't you go into the supermarket?"

"I was going to, but I noticed a woman in there who I'm sure is Amanda Armitage, and considering her reputation, I thought I'd be less conspicuous in Haighs'."

Lisa tutted. "Well, as young Ivan was trying to tell you, the post box is inside the supermarket. It caught fire once too often out here. So if you don't want Mandy to recognise you, then turn up your coat collar. Now if you'll excuse me..."

"Yes. Of course. Sorry. I'll, er, I'll drop the three pounds off at the Health Centre later."

But Lisa was already gone, walking towards a red Ford Fiesta, the keys in her hand.

Baldock watched her shapely behind, wiggling as she strode to the car, where she bent to unlock the door. Lurid thoughts, prompting memories of teenage years when Lisa had been one of the most captivating girls on the estate, impinged upon his brain. He physically shook his head and frowned inwardly. There were times when he felt he had got close to her twenty years ago, but not *that* close, and he had not come back to Midthorpe to seek that which he had never found here as a youngster.

Turning the other way, striding towards the supermarket, the inherent lust in the way he had stared after Lisa was subdued not so much by his sense of purpose, i.e. posting two letters, but by the prospect of Amanda Armitage.

Mandy was a little older than his thirty-six years, and during those formative adolescent times when he had been maturing on the estate and lusting after the nubile Ms Yeoman, her reputation had been legendary.

"And mostly horizontal," he muttered to himself as he arrived at the supermarket entrance.

Large enough for the needs of a council estate, not large enough to draw in hordes of traffic from other areas, the place had always been a supermarket, but it had undergone many incarnations, even during the years he lived here. Now it was owned and run by a national chain, but it did not appear any the busier. Baldock peered in through the closed door and saw it was almost empty. He could not see more than one or two customers which was probably right for ten o'clock on a Friday morning. It would be busier in the afternoon when the mothers or unemployed fathers collected their offspring from school, but for now a young redhead pottered with a display of sweets near the checkout, and further back, near the tall chillers, he could see someone else stacking soft drinks into the chillers.

There was no sign of Mandy, so he stepped in and the redhead, no older than about eighteen or nineteen, turned and greeted him with a smile baring her nicotine stained teeth.

"Post box?" he asked.

She nodded to the right of the door through which he had just entered. He turned, looked, and there, as promised, was the post box, with Mandy's grinning form standing alongside it.

She had maintained her busty figure of two decades previously. Slightly bulkier in all areas, but still displaying a deep cleavage under her work wear, she had not lost the habit of showing off more leg than was strictly decent for a woman employed in a supermarket.

Not only working there, Baldock noticed, but according to the badge above her left breast, managing the place.

There was no mistaking the meaning behind her broad smile. She recognised him, and any second now she was about to announce it to the world… or that part of the world inhabiting the supermarket at this hour.

He quickly considered his options. Should he smile indulgently, pretending he thought her mentally deficient? Or should he ignore her altogether, drop his envelopes in the post box and be on his way?

"Look what the cat dragged in."

Her announcement, packed with salacious humour, left Baldock with no option. He nodded stiffly. "Ms Armitage."

"Cowling. And it's Mrs Cowling. I've been wed to Graham these last fifteen months." She flashed her ring finger at him, laden with ostentatious jewellery. "So what brings the famous Raymond Baldock here?"

"I have to post these letters," he explained, and dropped the envelopes in the box.

"You came all the way back to Midthorpe to post two letters? Don't they have post boxes in Sussex?"

"Norfolk," he corrected her. "No, of course I didn't come back here to post letters. I have business here."

"Ooh. Business. What kinda business?"

Baldock stood up straight, stared her in the eye. "No business of yours." He turned for the door.

He stepped out into the summer sun once again, and took a deep breath. Two ghosts from his past, three if you counted young Haigh (although he did not remember the shopkeeper from his youth) and he had dealt with them. All right, so he had not been devastating, he had not crushed them or compelled them to heed his very presence, but he had scored points from Mandy Armitage, held his own against Haigh, and only to Lisa Yeoman had he yielded some ground. A promising start.

He made his way back to the roadside outside Haighs and climbed behind the wheel of his silver-grey Mercedes. Time to meet with Mother.

***

Letting herself into her office at the Health Centre, Lisa dropped her briefcase on the floor close to her desk, and flopped into the chair.

"Raymond bloody Baldock," she said to the empty room.

Switching on the computer, she ran through her day's appointments. Full. The first client, a young woman desperate to give up smoking before her unborn child arrived, would come through the door in the next ten minutes, and from then up to four o'clock, Lisa would have no time to herself.

She had not recognised Baldock right away. Queuing behind him in Haigh's she had been conscious only of her anxiety to get to work, and she was already late. She liked half an hour to herself before starting on the day's workload and the nitpicking with Ivan Haigh was eating into that breather. But once he declared, 'I am Raymond Baldock, the novelist', the memories came flooding back.

Some were happy, some were sad, but mostly they were of absolute frustration at his obdurate and painstaking nature; exactly as he had behaved in the shop. The world had to bend to the will of Raymond Baldock.

But of course, it did not, and he had never been able to understand why. In the same class throughout their days at Midthorpe Primary, he could not comprehend why others did not hang on his every word. It seemed incredible to him that they were more interested in games of hide and seek than the precise distance from the Earth to Jupiter as determined by the latest orbital telescopes. He was frequently beaten up by other boys, and sometimes by the girls, but still he could not see why, still he did not drop that haughtiness which tried to assume command; tried and failed.

And when he won his scholarship to the prestigious Headingley School, matters got worse. He would pontificate, he would try to educate whether or not his audience wanted it.

Even so, as he grew into a tall, athletic teenager, there were those girls who found him impressive and attractive, and Lisa made no apologies for being one of that small number.

With the benefit of her own higher education, a grounding in psychology and her later training as a general counsellor, it was easy for her to see what was wrong with him. He never played. As a child he never played in the street. A houseful of toys, shared with his elder brother, had never interested him. Only his books. And few of those were fiction. Aside from a fascination with James Bond, most of his reading tended to be biographies or encyclopaedias, and at school, both Midthorpe and Headingley according to him, he preferred solo to team sports; activities such as cross-country running or long-distance track events. He had to be pressed into the rugby, football and cricket teams, and invariably came away with some kind of minor injury.

Since his emergence as a successful novelist almost a decade previously Lisa had followed his career with an interest bordering on obsession. She had seen or heard him numerous times on TV and radio, and still he had not lost that inherent tone of superiority in his voice. If anything Cambridge had reinforced it to the point where she felt his arrogance would qualify him as a modern politician.

Raymond Baldock was clear and determined about everything, and the one aspect of his character which she knew had come from Midthorpe, was his habit of telling it bluntly and as it was... or as he saw it. His view, coloured by an unhappy youth on Midthorpe did not always coincide with reality, but he refused to court popularity, and even those journalists prepared to admit that they did not like him, nevertheless commended his candour.

"He might be a pompous prat," said the literary reviewer from one of the weekend broadsheets, "but at least he's an honest pompous prat."

Most of all, Lisa remembered a shy seventeen-year-old who blushed when he kissed her, who steadfastly showed no interest in fondling her burgeoning breasts, or placing his hands on her bottom to crush her closer to him. And a year later, bursting with nervous excitement, he went off to Cambridge, taking his very presence from her, when what she really wanted was for him to take her before he left.

Chapter Three

Midthorpe estate was tagged onto South Leeds almost as an afterthought.

Built in the 1920s to house the families of the men who worked at the now-defunct Midthorpe Colliery, the estate appeared broadly apple shaped when viewed on a map, and Midthorpe Avenue ran north to south through the exact centre.

Off to either side as Baldock drove down from the shops, were labyrinths of streets, some short, some longer, some cul-de-sac, others through roads. The Nimmons, named after some family that had owned most of the land during the early days of the Industrial Revolution, were to his right, and the Midthorpes sat to his left. He had been brought up in a two-bedroomed house on Midthorpe Terrace, where his mother still lived.

The Terrace was a strange street: a cul-de-sac at both ends, but it was unevenly split by the inappropriately named, one-mile long Midthorpe Walk passing through the middle. From the Walk, one could turn north into the Terrace (Nos 11-52) or south, (Nos 1-10). Turning left off the Avenue onto the Walk, Baldock next turned right, into the southern part of the street, drove down to the frying pan, and stopped outside No. 1.

This house, where he had grown up, faced straight up the street and from the upper front window, which had been his bedroom, he could see the two houses across the top of the northern half of the Terrace. Throughout his childhood, it had lent him a restricted and uninspiring view of the world. Other than when they flashed past on Midthorpe Walk, he could not see people, cars, vans, buses or lorries going about their business. Paradoxically, he often credited his superior intelligence to the siting of the house. If he had lived, for example, on the Avenue or even the Walk, there may have been more in the way of distractions from the outside world. As it was, he had had little to do but sit in his room, reading and learning.

His major concern now was the lack of a driveway at his mother's house. Midthorpe had a reputation for low-level crime, and he did not like the thought of his Mercedes – several cuts above the usual vehicles found on the estate – parked on the street.

He climbed out of the car, pushed open the gate and as he did so, the front door opened and his mother, Janet, appeared, beaming her generous smile upon him.

She was, of course, expecting him. Emails and telephone calls had flitted back and forth between Wroxham and Leeds over the last few weeks until all the arrangements were sorted. He was ostensibly there for just a few days, having been invited to speak to GCSE candidates of Midthorpe Comprehensive School, but he had another, altogether different reason for coming home, and it was a point that would require delicate handling.

Returning to the car, he fished into the boot and took out his small suitcase. It contained only his immediate requirements and sufficient clothing to last for four or five days. Life on Midthorpe had taught him that he preferred not to be there at all, and if worst came to worst and he ended up having to stay for any length of time, he would have to go home to pick up clean clothing, but as matters stood, he had no plans to stay longer than the weekend.

Following his mother into the house, he automatically turned left into the kitchen, where she assured him the kettle would be coming to the boil. He found himself a mixture of emotions. There was the undeniable pleasure of seeing his mother again, mixed with a deep wave of nostalgia, countered by a matching surge of near-revulsion and panic, mentally yelling at him demanding to know what he was doing back on this dreadful estate, and bidding him to get out while he could.

He suppressed it all, dropped his case by the bottom of the stairs, and sat at the Formica topped table while his mother attended to the kettle.

"I shouldn't leave your car there, Raymond. The thieving so-and-sos round here will have the fancy wheels off it before you know it."

"They're alarmed, Mother," he assured her. "Besides, it's a little difficult to leave it anywhere else. You don't have a drive."

"I've never had a car. Not since your father… er… you know." Janet sat opposite her son and poured tea from a novelty ceramic pot shaped like a London Bus and bearing the logo of the 2012 Olympics. She noticed him studying its absurd, grotesque shape and artwork. "A friend bought it for me when we were down there for the track and field events," she explained.

"Quaint," Baldock said, mustering as much sincerity and enthusiasm as he could. It was not much.

"Did you have a good journey?" Janet asked.

"Tiring," he replied. "I left my house at six this morning. It's hard work until you get onto the A1 near Newark. In total, it took me about four hours. I was in Haigh's, at the top of Midthorpe Avenue just after ten o'clock."

"Mr Haigh had to retire, you know. Stroke. Young Ivan's taken over."

"So I noticed." Baldock frowned. "Can't say I remember young Haigh, and yet I don't think I'm much older than him."

"He always had to help his dad in the shop after school, so he didn't mix. Neither did you. Not really."

"No, but I don't remember him from school."

"A good few years behind you, Raymond."

Janet sipped at her tea, and Baldock sipped at his.

He was almost embarrassed at the silence. On the long drive up from the far side of Norwich, he had rehearsed all the things he and his mother would talk about when they were together. He had not seen her since the Christmas before last, and even then she had met him at a restaurant in Leeds. There was a lot of catching up to be done, but now that he was here, now that he was sitting with her, he couldn't recall any of it.

"I bumped into…"

"So how are you…"

They forced smiles at the simultaneous attempts to strike up conversation.

"Go on, Raymond," Janet invited.

"I was about to say I bumped into Lisa Yeoman in Haigh's. She's some kind of counsellor, I believe."

Janet nodded. "Hmm, yes. At the Community Health Centre. She has her own flat in Leeds, you know, but her dad still lives on Nimmons Crescent. Behind the old dairy.

"She saved my bacon in Haigh's," he confessed, and went on to explain what had happened in the shop.

"Oh, Raymond, if you're short of money—"

"I'm not short of money, Mother. I was short of cash. I'll have to drop into the Centre and pay her back." Realisation dawned on him and he dug into his pocket for a notebook. "While I think about it, can you give me your bank details?"

Suspicion haunted her eyes. "Why?"

"Well, I keep sending you cheques, Mother, and it would be easier if I could pay the money direct into the bank. And you want more off me this time. I know I'm only here for a few days, but I'm not staying for free, am I? I couldn't put on you like that. If you give me your bank account details, I'll transfer some money into your account. Shall we say five hundred pounds instead of the usual four hundred?"

"Oh. Yes. Isn't that a bit too much?"

"It's less than I'd pay for a hotel in the city centre, and I'm not a teenage student any more, Mother. I can afford it."

"All right, dear. If you insist." Still, Janet appeared uncertain.

"So what's the problem?"

"My bank details. They're always warning us not to give out our details, Raymond."

"That's to total strangers, Mum. I'm your son. I'm not

going to rob you of your life's savings."

Janet's discomfort increased. "I'd rather have a cheque, like normal. If it doesn't put you out."

"Well. I don't see—"

"It's the housing benefit, you see. If you can give me a cheque, I can pay it into my second account. The one they don't know about."

Baldock only just prevented his jaw from dropping. "What? Are you... Mother, I've been subsidising your income for years." He hurried on in case she misunderstood him. "I don't mind. You're my mother and I won't see you in poverty. But you can't claim benefits while I'm sending you money. It's fraud."

"Yes, but it gets so terribly complicated, Raymond. And I have told you I don't need the extra money. It's welcome, of course, but you don't have to do it. But it does get confusing, what with you in Northwich and—"

"Norwich," he interrupted.

"Yes, dear. It's all so complicated. On the other hand, if I don't say anything, they don't know and everyone is happy, and it's not like I'll be claiming thousands and thousands, is it? Only a few pounds a month."

Bewilderment threatened to overtake him. "Mother, it doesn't matter if it's five pounds or five thousand, it's benefit fraud. You can be prosecuted for it. You can go to prison for it."

"Yes but when they speak to me, I just put on my puddled old lady act and they leave me alone. They think I have Oppenheimer's."

"You mean Alzheimer's."

"I know, but when I call it Oppenheimer's they're even more convinced I have Alzheimer's." Janet reached across the table, and patted the back of her son's hand. "Be a good lad and just write me a cheque."

"All right. I'll attend to it." He sighed. His hidden agenda. The perfect time to broach it had just arrived. "Mother, this is all part of the reason I came here."

"To sort out my finances? I'm all right, Raymond.

Besides, I thought you were speaking to the school children."

"No, not your finances. And I'm speaking to the children this afternoon."

"Oh." Janet was obviously all at sea.

"I wanted to talk to you about moving."

"You're moving?"

Baldock was not listening. He was busy rehearsing his approach for the umpteenth time. "To Wroxham."

"I thought you lived there already."

"I do."

"Then why are you talking about moving there?"

He came to his senses. "Not me. You."

"Me?"

"Yes, Mother. I have a large house… a very large house, and there's a self-contained granny flat attached to it. You'd have your privacy, you'd be able to come and go as you please, entertain the new friends you'd make, and I'd have some peace of mind, not having to worry about you. Naturally, you could live there rent free."

"I live here rent free."

"No. The taxpayers pay your rent."

"It's the same thing from my point of view. Raymond, I think it's a lovely offer, but I've lived in this house ever since I married your dad, and I really don't want to live anywhere else." A distant sadness encompassed her fine features. "And now, with your brother gone and your father gone, all my memories are here, in this house, in this street." A tear glistened in the corner of her eye. "When I think of our Keith and you father…"

"Why are you speaking about them as if they're dead? It's very annoying. You know perfectly well that Keith is living in Manchester with his latest wife or girlfriend and Dad is in York, shacked up with the blonde who used to work in the bookies at the top of Midthorpe Avenue."

"Yes, Raymond, I know. But what can a thirty-year-old trollop offer your father that I couldn't? One day, he'll come knocking on that door begging me to take him back. And he won't be able to do that if I move to Wrexham, will he?"

"Wroxham, not Wrexham." Baldock felt as if he was swimming in a sea of confusion and he was in danger of going under. "It's been three, four years, Mum. And you'd still take him back?"

"Would I hell as like. But I'd love to see him come crawling back to that door, just so I could kick him in the nuts and watch him hobble away again."

Baldock's ears coloured. "Kick him in the… for goodness sake, Mother, do you have to resort to the language of the gutter?"

"Oh, don't be so snooty, Raymond."

"I'm not being snooty. One simply does not expect to hear one's mother—"

"Using the same industrial language as your father did?" Janet interrupted. "You are being snooty. You've been the same ever since you got those A levels and went off to Cambridge. You went all hoity-toity on us."

"I did not go hoity-toity." Baldock, conscious that he probably had become hoity-toity. He was fully on the defensive now, and felt as irritated with himself as he did with his mother. "I never fitted in on Midthorpe. Even as a boy, I had very few friends."

"Because you always had your nose stuck in a book, didn't you? Life isn't in books, Raymond. Life is what happens around you. Where were you when the other teenage boys were taking their birds and bees lessons from Mandy Armitage? Reading James bloody Bond and trying to work out why he was so interested in women's breasts." Janet shook her head sadly. "I blame your father. He should have sat down and had a long talk with you."

Her words prompted involuntary memories of teenage life with his parents, and his father's often disparaging views on the youngest Baldock boy.

"The only things my father ever talked to me about were Leeds United, the price of a pint, and the chances of his horses coming in. And I wasn't interested in any of them."

"At least he knew what women's breasts were for."

"Particularly the breasts on the blonde from the bookies."

Believing he had made his point, Baldock allowed a few moments of silence while he rehearsed his next words.

"Mother, I didn't come back to argue about my childhood. It was as it was and nothing is going to change that. I was glad to get away from this god-awful place. Three years at Cambridge did me the power of good. Without it, I wouldn't have got my first job as a staff writer and reviewer for *Sleuth Monthly*, and without that, I'd never have come up with the idea for Detective Inspector Richard Headingley, and without Headingley, I wouldn't have all that money in the bank."

"And is that all it's about, Raymond? Money?"

"Of course. I lead a free and comparatively easy life. For the most part, I do as I please and not what others insist I should do. I am my own man, beholden to no one."

"Right down to voting Conservative."

"My politics are my own affair, but yes, I see the Tories as the only credible option for forming a government."

Janet shook her head and tutted. "And you brought up in a solid mining area where everyone votes Labour."

"Being in a minority has never troubled me in the past, and it doesn't now," he insisted. "Mum, Midthorpe is a dump of the worst kind. I've heard it described as the anus of Leeds, and I can't fault that argument."

"That anus of Leeds?" Janet's brow furrowed. "I've heard it called the arsehole of Leeds, but never the anus."

"The anus is the arsehole," Baldock told her. "I moved away and I'm glad I did. I'd like you to move away, too."

Janet tutted and cradled her beaker in her delicate hands. "You have such a downer on this estate."

"With good reason."

"Yet it's such a lively place." She put the beaker down again. "I'm surprised you haven't set one of your novels here."

"What? Richard Headingley on Midthorpe? I don't think so. He may be a contradiction inasmuch as he's a police officer with intelligence, but I can't see him being bothered with trivia like stolen bicycles and routine burglaries."

"Oh, but there's so much more to Midthorpe, dear. We

have our share of bigger mysteries, you know. Look at young Nathan Perry."

Baldock frowned. "Nathan Perry? One of the Perry's from Nimmons Grove?"

Janet nodded as she swallowed mouthful of tea. "He's only sixteen years old, too. I went to school with his grandma, you know. Carol."

Baldock refused to be side-tracked into reminiscence. "So what about him?"

"Her, dear. Carol is a her."

"No, Mother, Nathan Perry. What about him?"

"Oh. Well, he disappeared, didn't he? Five months now. Early January. Went out to meet his friends one evening and never came back. And his friends say he never turned up to meet them."

Baldock's memory clicked into place. "It made the national news, believe it or not. In fact, it's half the reason I ended up coming here to speak to these children."

Janet waited for him to go into more detail, but he did not.

"He just disappeared did he? Did anyone check the police cells?"

It was the kind of casual sneer for which Baldock was renowned, especially when it came to Midthorpe, but at the back of his mind, he was already trying to weave the disappearance of the young man into a Headingley novel.

Thanks to the efforts of Shortly Publishing and his agent, Bernie Deerman, his books had been a runaway success, and made him one of the country's best-selling authors. Headingley had a hardcore group of fans who would buy a postcard written by the fictional detective, and the planned TV series, which would go into production later in the year, had added to the fervour.

But beyond those followers, the critics were already sharpening their knives, declaring the series repetitive and unimaginative. 'Routine whodunits, with a misogynist copper who considers women as a hindrance except when they're dropping their knickers for him' was the opinion of one columnist.

While impervious to such criticisms – Baldock insisted he was turning out what readers wanted – he had to admit that his own tastes would never allow him to reading pulp fiction like the Headingley novels, but the notion of the great detective being called upon to follow up a missing teenager on a council estate might silence the critics while pushing up the readership numbers.

Making a mental note to speak to Bernie about it, he pushed these thoughts to the back of his mind and pressed his mother again.

"I'd like to see you come away from this place. You deserve better than Midthorpe, and a son's duty is to ensure his mother gets only the best."

"I have lived here all my life, Raymond. I have no wish to live anywhere else. Besides, I have the Tenant's Association to consider. I'm the charwoman."

Baldock felt his anger rise. "What? You're cleaning for some low-life, council run organisation? I'll—"

Janet interrupted with a laugh. "Sorry. I meant Chairwoman. The Association rely on me."

Baldock sulked again. "And what, precisely, do they get up to?"

"We arrange outings for children, bingo sessions at the old peoples' home, and naturally, we canvass the council on matters that need their attention. We have a lot of boomers amongst our membership."

"Boomers as in—"

"Baby boomers. Born between 1946 and 1964. All old gits. And right now, Raymond, I am one of those old gits." A new enthusiasm burned into Janet's voice. "While I think on, I must tell you, I shall be away tonight. We're going to Leeds this evening to see Fifty Shades of Grey."

Once again, Baldock was appalled. "Fifty Shades of... what? You do know that that movie is not about choosing paint for the living room?"

"Of course I do. I only hope it's as good as the book."

"Mother!!!"

She ignored his outrage. "I could come home, but some of

us fancied making a night of it, so we're staying overnight in the city."

"In a hotel, I hope?"

"Well we're not dossing under cardboard round the back of the railway station, are we? Shared rooms, obviously. We don't all have the funds to pay for single rooms." Janet smiled coyly. "I'll be with a friend."

Baldock missed the tiny inflection in her voice. "As long as you're not alone."

"You'll have to fend for yourself tonight, Raymond."

"I'm used to it, Mother." He finished his tea and stood up. Picking up his suitcase, he asked, "Which room am I in?"

"Your old room. At the front."

"In that case, I'll unpack and then whip round to the Health Centre to repay Lisa Yeoman before I go to the school… And while I think about it you'd better tell me how to get to both the Health Centre and the school. I don't know either."

"You can give Lisa's money to me if you like. I'll be seeing Tim tonight and he'll make sure Lisa gets it."

Baldock shook his head. "No. That's okay. I'd like to see her again."

Chapter Four

Baldock's visit to Midthorpe Community Health Centre was unproductive. The receptionist phoned through, and then reported back that Lisa was busy all afternoon, and if he really wished to speak to her, he would have to come back after four o'clock.

Grumbling to himself on the unyielding rigidity of the NHS, he drove back towards his mother's house, but instead of turning into the Terrace, carried on along Midthorpe Walk to its natural end half a mile further on, where he came to the gates of Midthorpe Comprehensive School. Parking his car outside, he climbed out, and looked at the land either side of the building.

Beyond the perimeter in either direction were open fields, just as he recalled them from his youth. To the south, far away, he could see traffic moving on the M62 and a build-up of queuing vehicles where the trans-Pennine motorway met the M1. He fervently wished he was in that queue. At least it would be taking him away from this awful estate.

The school was a squat agglomeration of concrete and slate-grey breeze block. Unlike many modern schools, there was no vast expanse of glass. Midthorpe and large windows were a mixture every bit as lethal as electricity and water, and as he stepped into the building through a pair of wooden, double doors, it occurred to him that someone must have thoroughly briefed the architect on the Midthorpe reputation.

When he was growing up on the estate, the school did not even exist. Back then, children came out of Midthorpe Primary and the following year, entered Midthorpe Secondary, across the playing fields. Baldock never had. His diligence had seen him win a place at Headingley School where the more middle class pupils looked down upon scholarship boys like him, but where he had once again excelled and eventually secured his place at Cambridge. He was so grateful to Headingley School that he had named his hero detective after the place.

Back in those far off days, the fields confronting him were one of the areas where the Midthorpe teenagers learned the basics of sex – often with Mandy Armitage – and where the illicit lovers honed those rough and ready skills to something approaching perfection… or whatever passed for perfection on Midthorpe. Baldock recalled some of the tales his peers had told of their exploits in those fields, and with some degree of disappointment recalled that he never had any exploits to tell of. He had lost his virginity to a nubile tramp from Stoke-on-Trent whom he met in his first year at Cambridge, a young woman who seemed determined to sleep her way through the entire intake of Freshers.

Stepping into Midthorpe Comprehensive, where he might expect to find a large, highly polished roll of honour and gowned senior master waiting to greet him, he was confronted instead with a conventional reception counter where the middle-aged attendant smiled politely, asked him to sign in as a visitor and then sent for the teacher concerned, who appeared a few minutes later.

"You're a Midthorper, I believe?" Terry Hardwick asked as they shook hands.

"It's not something I boast about," Baldock replied.

Hardwick, he guessed, would be about the same age as himself, but where sensible eating and regular exercise, particularly in the gym, had enabled Baldock to maintain a trim figure, Hardwick was already spreading at the waist. His pale pink shirt flopped over the waistband of a cheap suit, his tie was hooked down from the collar and his top shirt button was undone. As they made their way along a corridor stinking of floor-cleaner, Baldock, who prided himself on his luxurious head of neatly trimmed, dark hair, also noticed that the man's sandy and untidy mop was thinning at the crown.

"I take it you're not from the estate?" Baldock asked.

It was not that he was particularly interested, but the

corridor appeared never-ending, and Hardwick was taking them all the way to infinity. Chitchat was preferable to complete silence.

"Married a Midthorper." Hardwick laughed sardonically. "Just my luck, eh? Elaine Perry as she was when I met her. Fact is, I'm not even from Leeds, never mind Midthorpe. Huddersfield, originally, but I did my teacher training here in Leeds and put in some of my training hours at this school. When I graduated, the vacancy came up and I went for it." He shrugged and stopped outside a classroom, one hand on the doorknob. "It's a living."

"So is digging holes in the road, and frankly I'd rather do that than your job." Baldock nodded at the door. "Your class. Do they live up to the Midthorpe reputation?"

"Somewhat. Year eleven. Final year for GCSEs and they're in the middle of exams right now. Some of these kids are good. They'll go on to sixth-form college and maybe uni'. As for the rest… well, they're mostly old school. All they want is to get out of this place. Maybe they fancy digging holes in the road. They're under parental pressure to bring a wage into the house."

"I remember it," Baldock admitted. "I came under the same pressure, but only from my father."

"You ignored it, obviously."

"If you'd ever met my father, you'd understand why."

Hardwick chuckled. "What we're hoping, Raymond – you don't mind if call you Raymond, do you – is that you can show them the benefits of higher education. After all, you're a Midthorper. You came from a working class family, just like them, and you made good. Better than good, if the *Sunday Times* is anything to go by."

"I make a lot of money, true, but there's more to my story than that."

"Then let's tell 'em."

Hardwick pushed open the door and led the way in.

Baldock spent the next two hours in the company of twenty teenagers, most of whom he managed to bore within five minutes, much to his own confusion. In his time at

Headingley, and more so at Cambridge, he had attended talks by some quite famous people; politicians, church leaders, sportsmen and women, actors and writers, and the leaders of industry. He had even had his photograph taken with a former Chancellor of the Exchequer. He never found the lectures boring. These were people who had succeeded in life. Some of them came from quite humble backgrounds, and yet they had outstripped their peers and contemporaries through their single-minded determination to reach the top. What was boring about that?

"It's not gonna happen for most of us, is it?" replied one girl when he put the question to the group. "We're from Midthorpe. That automatically pushes you five steps down the ladder before you've even put a foot on it."

"I'm from Midthorpe, too. My mother still lives here and I'm guessing I know many of your parents. Yet, I made it."

A young man at the rear of the room threw his feet up on the desk. "Yeah, but you sucked up to the teachers, didn't you? My old man told me all about you."

Baldock searched the database of faces in his memory, in an effort to match the black, unruly hair and contemptuous curl of the lips.

"Do you put your feet on the table at home?"

"Yep."

"Then it's a good job you don't live with me, because I'd cut them off at the ankles." Baldock stared at the trouser cuffs, stained with a pale cream, paste-like substance. "And don't you ever wash your clothes?"

"Me mam does 'em... but she's working."

Baldock reached a match in his mind. "You're Lipton, aren't you?"

The young man gawped. Alongside him, his dark-skinned friend grinned broadly.

"And you're Billy Allen's son, aren't you?"

The grin disappeared.

"You see, just because I've made a lot of money and become comparatively well-known, it doesn't mean I've forgotten my roots." Striding between the desks, pausing to knock Lipton's feet from the desk, Baldock did not add that he wished he *could* forget his roots. "I went to school with both your fathers. Your dad bullied me, Lipton, but I had the last laugh. And your father, young Allen, suffered as much discrimination as me, but it was because of the colour of his skin, whereas I was ostracised because I believed in hard work."

"Toughened my dad up," Josh Allen declared.

"It toughened me up, too." Baldock returned to the front of the group. "After Midthorpe Primary, there was nothing in this world to fear, and I'm back here today not even afraid of the bullies who attended Midthorpe Primary in my childhood."

"Bet you wouldn't say that to my dad," Lipton snapped. "He'd smite you."

"When we're through here, ring him, tell him to meet me and I will say it to him."

It was just after three when they called it a day. None of the students could think of any serious questions for him and they dispersed, leaving him with Hardwick.

"Sorry about Lipton," the teacher apologised as he escorted Baldock to the staff common room for a cup of tea. "He's a smart lad, but he has this attitude problem."

"He probably got it from his father, but if he's smart, that must come from his mother."

A little under an hour later, they shook hands and parted at the main entrance. Baldock stepped out into bright, afternoon sunshine, ambled through the gates, and unlocked his car door.

Climbing behind the wheel, he started the engine, slotted the transmission into reverse, and let the parking brake off.

The car did not move. He put it into neutral and again into reverse and still it did not move. Thinking he may be stuck in mud, even though he was on concrete, he gunned the gas, and nothing happened other than a loud scraping noise from the rear. He killed the engine and climbed out. Only then did he look at his rear wheel and find it missing, while the hub and axle rested on a pile of house bricks.

***

Once his wheel was replaced, Baldock retraced his earlier route to the Midthorpe Community Health Centre, just off the Avenue opposite Midthorpe Primary School.

Climbing out of his car, he gazed first at the school, an agglomeration of redbrick buildings, with large, tarmacked play areas in front, spread across a couple of hundred yards. Beyond the labyrinth of buildings was the vast sports field, and beyond that, Midthorpe Secondary Modern, the buildings a mirror image of the primary school.

Looking on Midthorpe Primary, which he had first entered at the age of five, his memories seemed to be lost in the mists of time, but on those rare occasions when he did recall the years there, it was not with any fondness. The teachers were fine, helpful and encouraging, but the other boys and girls were nothing short of hostile; spiteful and mean to anyone who did not adhere to the strict protocol of play, waste your time reading comics, and be as disruptive as possible in class. Naturally, Baldock did not fit that template, and neither had he ever wanted to.

In the long run, he had got it right, and that gave him some satisfaction. Headingley had prepared him for Cambridge, which in turn had prepared him for the real world of commerce and enterprise, and *that* had paid off handsomely. He was worth a fortune. What were all those other children, most of them inattentive plebs, doing with their lives? Digging holes in the road, as he had suggested to Hardwick, or stocking shelves in supermarkets like Amanda Cowling-nee-Armitage, standing behind shop counters and making life difficult for others like Ivan Haigh, or worse still, eking out an existence on benefits which his taxes paid for.

Allowing his gaze to wander further from the school, he cast his mind back to the 80s and 90s, those years when he had been growing up in Midthorpe. Back in those far off days, there had been a library, a small police station and tenants' hall opposite the school. His brother's wedding reception had been held in the hall. It was now gone, and so was the library, but Baldock was surprised to see that the police station, a small, redbrick blockhouse, looking as if it had been transported from a military base, was still there, its large sign announcing its purpose, but its blue door closed, as if it was determined to demonstrate its presence while shutting out any possible contact with the locals.

He turned his attention to the four-storey Health Centre, a functional, glass and concrete construction, dominating everything; even the church next door. He had not considered the prospect of registering with a local GP. He did not use the local GPs in Wroxham. He had what amounted to something like a phobia of walking into an NHS waiting room and catching whatever germs and viruses the regular sick, lame and lazy clientele might be carrying. He would be here only for a few days and if he needed a doctor, he would pay for one.

He readily acknowledged that the acquired snobbery was totally at odds with his early, working class upbringing, but it complemented perfectly his opinion of those same working classes. And yet, he refused to accept that he was hoity-toity, as his mother put it. He had bettered himself. End of story.

Ensuring his car was locked, he made his way to the entrance, and as he did so, a bulky, figure came out through the automatic doors. The unshaven face grinned maliciously.

"So it's true, then? Ballcock is back."

The familiar, hated nickname forced a rush of blood to Baldock's cheeks. He brought it under control quickly, and feigning puzzled indifference, tried to sidestep, but the other man moved and blocked the way.

Identifying Peter Lipton had taken time. Recognising his father took no time, and in that instant, the years of bullying, intimidation and humiliation he had suffered at this man's hand came back to haunt him. Lipton had aged over the last twenty years, obviously, but there was still no mistaking the pugnacious face, and jet black hair, now furnished with a dark moustache and a two-day stubble.

Lipton would not let him pass, but Baldock was no eight-year-old boy now. He was a man, a successful man. He was taller than Lipton, in better physical condition and possessed of greater determination.

"Get out of the way. I've had enough of your family for one afternoon."

"So I heard. My lad rang me."

"And it's obvious he's a chip off the old block," Baldock growled. "You were a bully and a moron thirty years ago, and it's obvious that time has not helped you generate any more brain cells or manners. Chances are he'll continue the family tradition. Now kindly move out of the way so I can pass."

Lipton showed no inclination to do anything of the kind. "You just called me a moron."

"I was being generous. I didn't think you'd understand Neanderthal or troglodyte."

Lipton's fists clenched.

Baldock refused to back down. "Go ahead. I'm not the skinny little kid you used to beat up." He sneered into the malign, piggy eyes. "Give it your best shot."

***

Lisa guided Baldock's hand to the cotton-wool wad pushed into his left nostril. "Press here and hold. It should stem the blood in a few minutes." She tutted. "Really, Raymond, I thought you would have had more sense than to tackle Gary Lipton. He was a punch drunk prat when we were all in school, and he's still a punch drunk prat. Unless you know how to deal with it, you're best ignoring him."

"I've always believed that if you stand up to bullies, they back down." With one nostril closed, his voice sounded strange, even to him.

"Bullies with intelligence, or bullies who can be intimidated by a mob, yes. Lipton doesn't have much intelligence, and you're not a mob."

"Well, despite him besting me this time, I can't be intimidated either. I'll call at the police station on my way out."

"Waste of time. If Grunny is there, he won't do anything."

"Grunny? Steven Grunwell? He's the community constable?" Waiting for Lisa to confirm, Baldock wondered how many more surprises he could take in one day. "He'd just signed on with the police as I left for uni'. He was always bone idle."

"At least you remember him and what he was like." Lisa pushed the first aid trolley away. "Now remember, I'm a counsellor, not a nurse, so patching up your busted nose is a favour. When you called earlier, the desk said you'd asked for me. And here you are, back again. What is so urgent that you had to come back? And make it quick. I've had a long day and I'd like to get home."

"I came to repay the money I owe you. From Haigh's. This morning."

"Oh, that. There was no hurry."

"I like to keep the books straight. And anyway, I'm only here for the weekend."

He leaned forward and looked down at his crisp white shirt, now spattered with blood from his nose. It wasn't that Lipton had hit him particularly hard, either. It had more to do with the soft lining of his nasal cavities; a result of being forced to play rugby against his wishes when he attended Midthorpe Primary.

Ignoring the shirt – he would probably have to throw it away and buy new – he dug into his pocket and came out with three pound coins.

"You don't have the seventy eight pence?" Lisa asked.

"Sadly, not."

"I don't like owing you." A flash of doubt crossed her face, as if she felt Baldock might be affronted by her remark. "I don't like owing anyone."

"Then put the change in the charity box," he suggested.

A brief silence fell, and while Lisa put the money in her purse, Baldock toyed with different approaches. This next bit was the most difficult. It was something he should have done twenty years ago, but he had never found the courage. Three years at Cambridge, followed by his rapid success had steeled him for many situations, but even so, he felt nervous.

"Was there something else, Raymond?"

"Well, I, er—"

"Only like I said, I'd like to get finished and on my way home."

"Have dinner with me."

He blurted it out so fast that Lisa was stunned into silence, and even he did not have time to realise how abrupt he sounded. His cheeks and ears coloured, and he stammered to a more moderate request.

"That… that is, I'm, er, I'm on my own tonight. Apparently Mother is going to the cinema, and er…"

"Yes I know," Lisa said, taking advantage of another brief silence. "It's the Midthorpe over-fifties club. My dad's going too."

"Well, I thought we could perhaps…" He trailed off again, took a deep breath and got a hold of himself. "I've been back a few hours and I've seen no one who has a single, good word to say, other than you and my mother. I'd planned to take her out for a meal, but she obviously has alternative plans, and if you're alone…" His brow creased. "You are alone, aren't you?"

"If you mean am I married, the answer is no, am I in a relationship, the answer is still no. I never did marry and I've tried the relationship thing and it didn't work."

"Good. Well, not good that it didn't work, but good that you would be free to, er… only if you wanted, of course."

She smiled. "Yes, all right, Raymond. Where? Tell you what, The Midden do a smashing three course."

Encouraged though he was by her smile of acceptance, he was a little concerned at her choice of venue. "The Midden? The Midthorpe Hotel?"

"It's not like it used to be, Raymond. The tap room hasn't changed much, but the rest of the pub has gone upmarket, and the food is really good." She checked her watch. "At this hour on a Friday, you'd be hard pressed to get a table at the city's best restaurants, but you don't have to book at The Midden."

He elected to cut his losses. He did not fancy The Midden,

but at least he would be in her company. "Fine. Shall I pick you up or meet you there?"

"I'll meet you there. Eight o'clock?"

He nodded and stood up. "I'd better get home to mother's, and shower and change."

"Yes. Er, Raymond?"

"Yes?"

"Take the wadding out of your nose first."

***

On stepping out of the Health Centre, flushed with exhilaration and anticipation, Baldock ignored his throbbing nose, and after checking that all the wheels were in place on his Mercedes, made for the police station and found that, although the door was shut, it was not locked.

He found himself in a tiny reception area, dominated by a corkboard, littered with the usual notices on securing your car/bicycle/house against intruders, along with notifications of recent crimes intermingled with arrangements for local elections. Ahead of him was a sliding window of frosted glass, and through its distorted view he could make out a uniform-clad figure either seated or reclining, Baldock could not be sure which.

He pressed the buzzer and the figure moved. Many seconds passed before, with some barely-audible grunting, it climbed out of the chair and first attended to something off to the right before coming to the window and sliding it open.

Aged somewhere in his early forties, PC Steven Grunwell had changed little in the eighteen years since Baldock had left for Cambridge. His brown hair was a little thinner, and his face sagged a little more, but he was still tall, slender and lugubrious.

His attitude had not altered either, Baldock noted. The item Grunwell had attended to before coming to the window was the kettle, now happily coming to the boil. From the desk came the sound of children's afternoon television playing to itself, and in the background, the occasional burst of static from the police radio.

Grunwell scanned Baldock's face, pondered for a moment, and then his blue eyes brightened. "Well, slap me with a wet fish and bill me for the chips if it isn't Raymond Baldock. What are you doing back here?"

"Disturbing your afternoon nap, I think."

The community constable, who in Baldock's opinion had never been part of the community and had obviously amounted to nothing as a constable (or he would not have been allocated Midthorpe as his beat) did not appear irritated by the snide remark. "Yes, well, busy days, you know. Not much peace for the great and the good on Midthorpe. Too many scroats. So what can I do for young Baldock?" Grunwell concentrated his tired eyes on Baldock's bruised nose. "Been scrapping have you?"

"I had a slight altercation with Gary Lipton."

Grunwell tutted. "Not a wise move. Not for you anyway. You never could look after yourself in a fight. Better to avoid daft buggers like Gary." He yawned. "So knuckle sandwiches aside, is it just a social call? Looking for an old-fashioned beat bobby to put into one of your books, are you?"

"You'd make an interesting role model in one of the Headingley novels," Baldock admitted. "The inspector could use you as an example of what policing is not about."

"If you're here to—"

"I want to report a crime."

"Ah. Oh. Well, that's different."

Grunwell spent a few moments looking for the official forms, and then finding a pen that actually worked, then a little longer filling in the various headers; date, time, his identity.

While this was going on, Baldock glanced at the clock on the wall behind Grunwell. Four thirty-five. He needed to get back to his mother's, shower and change and he didn't really have time for Grunwell's lackadaisical approach.

"Right, so the nature of the crime?" Grunwell asked at last. "Punch up with Gary Lipton?"

"No. That's a personal matter and I'll deal with it my own

way. It's theft. Someone stole one of my car wheels while it was parked outside Midthorpe Comprehensive."

Grunwell put down his pen. "I see. And someone suggested you call here looking for a replacement, did they? Well, you know the old industrial units on Tansey Lane, at the bottom of the Avenue? There's a place there—"

"I've already had it replaced," Baldock interrupted, his mind suddenly filled with images of the tiny industrial estate on the road to the motorway.

"Then why are you telling me?"

Grunwell's question brought him back from the industrial units. "It's a crime. I'm reporting it."

"Why?"

"You're the police, aren't you? I mean it does say police outside. Or is that some kind of in-joke around Midthorpe? You're not really the law, just a local dole scrounger who pretends to be with the cops so the real police don't turn up and interrupt your daily round of sleep, *Jeremy Kyle*, sleep, *Loose Women* and more sleep."

Grunwell laid his palms flat on the counter, and raised himself upright. "Now listen here. That kind of attitude might be the way you speak to the law in Ambridge, but—"

"Cambridge. Ambridge is a fictitious town in *The Archers*. And I live near Norwich, not Cambridge. Now are you going to investigate or not?"

"Not." Grunwell's attitude softened a little "Y'see, it's the pressure of work. We're up to our eyes in it. I don't think I could find the time to check up on what is a routine and quite common occurrence round here. If you've have your wheel replaced, the best thing you can do is just forget about it and be about your business."

"At over five hundred pounds a wheel, I'm not willing to do that," Baldock retorted. "I'm reporting this matter, and I expect you to take the report seriously."

The constable scratched his forehead. "Not really sure what I can do. I could haul a few bodies in, give 'em the third degree, but to be honest, we'll have a list of suspects as long as your arm and all of them will have been in The Midden drinking with each other at the time of the alleged offence."

"Were you ever awake in English lessons, Grunwell? It's an actual offence, not alleged. It happened; it's real. One of my wheels went missing, and considering the rear axle was propped up on bricks, it obviously didn't fall off."

"All right, so I file your complaint. What makes you think you'll ever hear anything?"

Baldock sighed. "Just lodge the report and give me a crime number. At least that way I can claim against my insurance."

Grunwell began to fill out the forms while Baldock, filled with despair, watched the pen make its painstaking way back and forth across the paper, and consoled himself with the thought of a pleasant dinner in the company of Lisa Yeoman.

Chapter Five

"You're sure?" Janet asked.

Tim Yeoman nodded grimly. "I've checked all me pockets. Sorry, girl. I've forgotten them."

A few months younger than her, Tim was one of those men who looked after himself and as a result, even at the age of 65, he was still pleasant on the eye. No large, overhanging belly, no sagging jowls, and still blessed with a good head of hair. That he was diabetic had more to do with the shock of his wife's death a few years previously than obesity, which was the usual cause of the disease.

And yet, for all that, he was just as absent-minded as most men. Even when it came to the important things like...

Janet clucked irritably, and stared through the windows at the slow moving traffic over Leeds Bridge. "What are you like?"

"I'll have a word with Shippy," Tim promised with a nod at their driver. "He'll have something."

"No, it's all right. I'll speak to him when he drops us off. I have to pay him anyway."

The minibus belonging to and driven by Michael Shipston, was full: a dozen members of the Midthorpe Over-50s Club, looking forward to a movie and a night in Leeds.

It was an illegal taxi. Shipston was neither licenced nor insured for carrying passengers, but as with most things on Midthorpe, few people stopped to worry about it. He came cheap and that was the benchmark.

As Chair of the club, it was Janet's responsibility to ensure he was booked and, of course, paid for his work, and if she had any reservations about using an illegal service, they were soon quelled by the members, most of whom preferred to keep an eye on the purse strings rather than worry about trivia like insurance against accidents that were unlikely to happen.

Briggate, the main thoroughfare running through the heart of Leeds, was banned to all vehicles, and as a consequence, Shipston had to follow the bulk of traffic, turning right towards the rotunda of the Corn Exchange, and down past the Victorian edifice of Kirkgate Market, sticking to the Loop Road. Further down, where the traffic met other flows from the south and east, he skirted the bottom of the bus station before turning up Eastgate where the tall buildings on either side of the dual carriageway always reminded Janet of a scaled-down imitation of New York's Central Park West.

Not that she had ever been to New York, but she had been an avid fan of *Cagney & Lacey* in the 1980s.

A hundred yards on, Shipston stopped outside the Stannedge Hotel, on the opposite side of the street from the Gem Cinema, and killed the engine.

"Right, crumblies," he called out from the driver's seat, "this is as far as I go. I've got a hot pie and a hotter woman waiting for me at home, so move your clicky bones and get out. Janet, there's the small matter of money. Make a noise like fifty nicker coming my way… oh, and the rest of you, if you're looking for a few sweeties to help you try out some of the things in this fillum, come and talk to me. Fiver a dip, satisfaction not guaranteed, but a good time is."

As they dispersed onto the pavement, Tim and one or two other men taking small, overnight bags from the roof rack, Janet stood with Shippy, counting out five ten-pound notes into his hand.

"Oh, Michael, while I'm here, do you have any of those, watchemacallits? Fiagara toffees?"

Jamming the fifty pounds in one pocket of his jogging pants, casting a furtive glance up and down the road, ensuring there were no police nearby, Shippy dipped into the other pocket and came out with a small piece of bubblewrap secured with an elastic band. It had a large letter 'F' written on it in blue marker.

"As good as the real thing, but half the price. Just the one is it, Janet?"

She laughed. "How many times a night do you think we can manage at our age? Just the one."

"There you go, girl. To you, a fiver." He took the money and grinned. "Enjoy... hey, did I hear right? Raymond's in town?"

Janet waved up at the hotel. "Why do you think we're staying here for the night? We don't want our clicky bones falling on his delicate ears."

***

Where other areas of the Midthorpe had changed since his younger days, The Midthorpe Hotel, known locally as The Midden, had not. At least not on the outside, it hadn't. A large and imposing building, originally designed as a hotel and dance hall, it was synonymous with drink, crime and more drink on Midthorpe. It was often said that whatever you wanted, if you could not get it in the shops, it was usually to be found in The Midden, and that included buying back your own property, usually stolen from the people who stole it from you.

As a teenager, and particularly in his student days, when back in Leeds out of term, Baldock had never been particularly fond of the place, preferring to drink in the university quarter of North Leeds where he was at least guaranteed civilised company and intelligent conversation. In his opinion just about everything wrong with Midthorpe was to be found most nights propping up the bar in one of The Midden's three rooms.

He was pleased to learn, however, that after ignoring the tap room and passing through the large and crowded lounge, there was a pleasant and busy restaurant at the rear, where Lisa had already secured a table. Taking his seat, he ordered steak, well done for both of them.

"For health reasons, I prefer it very well done," Lisa told him.

"And I insist upon it in downmarket places." He cracked the cap on a bottle of still water.

While they waited for the food, Lisa asked, "Why have you come back, Raymond? Your mother?"

"Partly. As I told you, I want her to come and live with me in Wroxham. I think it would be better for her than Midthorpe. Certainly safer. She won't have her car wheels stolen in Wroxham."

"She doesn't own a car," Lisa pointed out.

"All right, so she won't have her theoretical car wheels stolen round Wroxham way."

Lisa took the gag with a sickly, forced grin. "And aside from your mother, the reason you came back is…?"

"My agent arranged for me to talk to the Year Eleven kids at the comprehensive."

Lisa's eyes brightened. "Ah, yes. I remember hearing that someone well-known was coming to talk to them. Good session?"

"Not so you'd notice. They were typical Midthorpe—"

"So you've found your way in here, have you?"

Cut off before he could tell Lisa more, Baldock looked up into Ivan Haigh's sardonic eyes.

His casual jacket did not fit him any closer than his shopkeepers overall had, and had the effect of making him appear comically fierce. A young blonde hung on his arm, smiling sweet recognition at Lisa.

"I suppose you own The Midden, too, do you?" Haigh asked.

"No, but I do have shares in the brewery," Baldock replied. "They don't get me any special treatment, but they do allow me to enjoy a meal in peace."

"Pardon me for breathing."

"You're pardoned as long as you don't breathe the same air as me. Now go away."

While Ivan and his young woman wandered off, Lisa's lips thinned and tightened. "Are you always so rude to people?"

"Only certain types of people."

"Midthorpers?"

"Mainly."

There was a brief and to Baldock's mind, irritated silence before Lisa spoke again.

"You were saying that the school talk didn't go well."

Baldock was glad of a return to the subject even though the memory still irritated him. "One or two of the kids appeared interested, but by and large they simply wanted to be out in the sunshine playing silly games on their phones." His features darkened. "And then there was Lipton junior. A real chip off the idiot block."

To his chagrin, Lisa disagreed. "I warned you about Lipton earlier, didn't I? Young Peter is different. Gary and his wife are separated and Peter lives with his mother. He's brighter, smarter than Gary ever was, but he still has these, er, influences in his life. Bad influences. He really needs a good, strong, guiding hand."

"Presumably you mean a hand that will not guide him to taking money from banks where he doesn't have an account?" Baldock snorted. "And people wonder why I hate Midthorpe so much."

It was a disparaging remark too far for Lisa. "For your information, Raymond, Gary turned away from petty crime years ago. He works for himself."

Baldock could not have been more surprised if she had told him that Lipton senior had entered a monastery. "He runs a business?"

"You remember he was always interested in cars?"

"I remember he stole enough of them to get him sent down a couple of times."

"Yes, well, that experience taught him enough about engines to get him a kosher job with a local company, and they trained him up. He was made redundant about ten years ago, and he used his settlement to set himself up. He has a small workshop on Tansey Lane. I don't think it makes a fortune, but he's living is honest, not hooky." She took a sip of tonic water. "What I'm trying to say, Ray, is that every town and city in the country has its Midthorpe. Even – where is it you live – Norwich."

"I don't live in Norwich, and you're probably right. But I grew up on Midthorpe, not any of the other scum estates." He made an effort to shift the subject slightly sideways. "Young Josh Allen was acting up this afternoon, too, and I couldn't understand that. I always liked Billy, and he suffered similar, er, discrimination as me."

"But Billy stayed here and fought back," Lisa said. "No one calls him because of his skin colour these days."

"Whereas, everyone welcomes me with open flick knives."

Their food arrived and as they ate, Baldock had to admit it was a well-prepared, good, wholesome meal such as he had enjoyed when he lived with his parents.

Diverting the conversational agenda to less controversial areas, as she chewed delicately on small pieces of beefsteak, Lisa asked, "When do you go home?"

"Monday. I promised Mother I'd stay for the weekend, but I have to be back to get on with the research for my next Headingley novel. It's to be set in a stately home outside Lowestoft."

"Have you ever thought of setting one on a council estate like Midthorpe?"

Baldock chuckled in what he hoped was not a condescending manner. "You're the second person to ask me that today. Forgive me, but Richard Headingley wouldn't really go well with a council estate. Have you, er, have you read any of them?"

"One, I think," she said. "Maybe two."

"You weren't impressed?"

"No. I thought they were very good, and obviously very popular."

Lisa fell silent and Baldock waited a few moments before giving her a verbal nudge.

"But?"

"I'm sorry?"

"Your tone indicated a 'but' after 'very popular'." Baldock explained.

"I was trying to think of the correct way of saying it, Raymond, without you assuming I'm trying to offend you."

He tried to sound offhand and casual. "I'm perfectly used to criticism, Lisa. You can say what you wish. I'm almost bulletproof."

"Very well. I found it a little too gory, too obsessed with the detail of dead bodies. It may be me, but I don't need such intricacy."

Baldock wore a fixed grin, telling himself that her words, 'did not get to him... did not get to him... did not get to him...'

Raymond Baldock has proven time and again that he has the knack of entertaining the gore-seekers, but he has yet to produce a work that will hold the attention of more erudite and discerning readers.

The opinion of a well-known critic rang through his head while Lisa waited for him to respond.

"Well, of course, there are a goodly number of adults who don't see such work as top drawer, but it would be impossible to please everyone."

Anxious not to get into deeper waters which might provoke an argument, he tactfully changed the subject, and through the remainder of the two courses, with the conversational hum of other diners and the clatter of knives and forks providing the ambience, they kept up a free-flowing stream of inoffensive conversation. She asked about his time at university, and after a lengthy account of his unadventurous years in Cambridge, he learned that after graduating from Manchester, she had lived in the Midlands for four years before returning to Midthorpe and taking her counselling qualification to settle into her job. A question on where he took his holidays (usually away from the high-profile resorts on either Majorca in the Balearics or Lanzarote in the Canary Islands) prompted him to throw the question back at her.

"I like the Costa Blanca," she declared. "I tend to go for either the quiet type of holiday in, say, Albir, or when I want to let my hair down, it has to be Benidorm."

Baldock wrinkled his nose. "Benidorm?"

"You should try it sometime. Go to places like Benidorm and Playa de Las Américas. See how the common people behave on foreign holidays." She invested the words 'common people' with heavy contempt.

Baldock managed to miss the sneer and once more felt a shockwave run through him. "You mean people from Midthorpe go on foreign holidays?"

"Well of course they do, Raymond. Your mother does. She must have sent you the odd postcard."

"I... er... Yes, yes, of course she did."

When success came, it was incumbent upon him to set up a PO Box for fan mail in an effort to separate it from business correspondence. As Lisa spoke, he recalled those sacks of mail, mostly handwritten, sent to the box. There had been occasional postcards in amongst the gushing sycophancy and sniping criticism, and he was certain some of those cards were fronted by images of foreign locations. Regardless, they had all gone straight into the recycling bin. Now, a wave of guilt ran through him. Was it possible some had been from his mother? And he had not read them?

"You always felt you were a cut above the rest of us, didn't you Raymond?"

Lisa's words brought him back from his appalled memories. He could sense her irritation rising.

"It wasn't a conscious thing." Even to himself he sounded apologetic.

"I'm not so sure. What were you doing while the rest of us were listening to Oasis, Celine Dion, even Chubby Brown singing *Living Next Door to Alice*? Tuning into Bach, Mozart, Beethoven and that kind of stuff."

"That's not true," Baldock argued. "I hate Mozart. And Beethoven. I'd much rather have Handel."

"You know what I mean."

Having had his fill of sticky toffee pudding, he pushed his dish to one side, dabbed at his lips with a napkin, and swallowed a mouthful of water.

"I said to my mother earlier today, I never fitted in on

Midthorpe. Never. I had very few friends. Billy Allen, I suppose, but we were never bosom buddies. There was only Ewan, really."

"Ewan Greaves?" Lisa shuddered at the mention of his name. "I never could stand him. He was always so..." She struggled to find the right word.

"Introverted?"

"Creepy."

Raymond blushed. "Yes, well, creepy or not, he was the only one I could call a real friend."

"And is he the friend who dragged you back up here? The one who spoke to your agent to get her to suggest you speak to the Year Eleven students?"

Now he chuckled. "Good lord, no. Ewan would not have the, er, wherewithal to do anything like that. To be honest, it was a casual remark I made to my agent. I was attending a book signing on Oxford Street—"

Lisa interrupted. "Oxford Street London. Not Manchester?"

"Of course London."

Despite his scornful tone, Lisa's annoyance had begun to calm as her interest rose. "So how did London's busiest shopping street prompt you to think of Midthorpe?"

"Only indirectly. We'd cried off for lunch and while we were in the nearest pub, the TV news said a young man from Midthorpe had gone missing. I just happened to mention I was from Midthorpe."

Lisa's face darkened. "When was this?"

"Early in the New Year."

"Nate Perry," she said grimly.

"Yes. My mother mentioned it earlier today. Never been seen since, apparently. I said to Bernie – did I mention she's my agent? Anyway, I said to her, that I came from Midthorpe and like me, the lad has probably had enough. Three weeks later she came up with the idea of me speaking to the schoolchildren here."

"And it took six months to organise it?"

"I have a very busy life, Lisa." Baldock wondered why he

was suddenly on the defensive. Switching the subject back, he said, "Anyway, if Nate Perry has left the area, all I can say is good for him. Most people here don't amount to anything."

"Whereas all those lost and homeless kids dossing near Kings Cross are really going up in the world, aren't they?"

The waiter came and took away the debris of their meal. Baldock took another sip of his water and waited until the table had been cleared before answering.

"Is there anything to indicate that he headed for London?"

"With its streets paved with gold, it's where most of them go. Tell you what I do think, Raymond. It would make an excellent investigation for someone with Richard Headingley's fine mind."

"I'll bear it in my fine mind." He smiled and got to his feet. "May I just say, I've actually enjoyed most of the evening. I don't think it's going to happen again, which is a pity, but you are excellent company, Lisa, and that's more than I can say for myself. If I've irritated you at all, then I'm sorry."

His cack-handed compliment caught Lisa slightly off her stride. "I, er, well, thank you, Raymond. Actually, you're not as bad as you make yourself out to be. You're certainly a refreshing change from the usual Midthorpers. Perhaps we could do it again, sometime. When you decide to make Headingley investigate the real world, instead of that of his upper class chums. You never know, maybe I could help you. At least give you the opposite point of view to Headingley's."

He beamed. "I'd like that. Give me a minute while I pay the bill."

As he left the table and crossed to the bar, he heard the trill of her mobile phone. A glance back revealed her looking through her bag for the instrument.

The attendant began to tot up the bill from the waiter's order, and while that was going on, Baldock's mobile gave out the theme tune from a blockbuster movie. Under the interested eye of the attendant, Baldock dug into his pocket and took out the phone. Checking the menu, he saw a number he did not recognise, but which began 0113, the dialling code for Leeds. Immediately he thought of his mother and while the attendant held out his hand for either payment or credit card, he made the connection.

"Raymond?"

"Is that you, Mother?"

"Yes. It is. I'm in a bit of a pickle and I wonder if you can help me out."

Pressing the phone to his ear and holding it there with a hunched shoulder, he took out his wallet and retrieved a credit card.

"I've been arrested."

Handing over the card and taking the phone in his hand once more, he chuckled. "Sorry, Mother, I was a bit busy. It sounded like you said you've been arrested."

"That is what I said. I've been taken to the police station at the bottom of The Headrow. I wondered if you could come down and sort it out."

Concentrating on the bar attendant, Baldock punched in his PIN to pay for his meal, and risked a glance back at Lisa who was gesticulating wildly and speaking angrily into her telephone. Whatever hopes Baldock had entertained for the remainder of the evening deserted him.

"Yes. All right, Mother. It'll probably take me half an hour to get to you."

"That's all right, luv. As long as I know you're coming."

Baldock took his receipt and credit card and turned away from the bar to find Lisa bearing down on him, her face flushed in fury.

"Right, Mother, I'll be there as soon as... Oh, I forgot to ask. Why have you been arrested?"

"Sexual assault and attempted murder."

Chapter Six

With the mobile pressed to his ear, Baldock was still reeling from the shock of his mother's admission, when Lisa squared up to him.

"What has your bloody mother done to my dad?"

"Raymond? Are you still there, Raymond?"

"That was Leeds General on the phone. My father is in A & E and he's seriously ill."

"Raymond? Who are you speaking to, Raymond?"

"Just because your rotten father walked out on Janet, doesn't give her the right—"

Finding it impossible to carry on two conversations at once, Baldock snapped out of his stupefaction. "I'll be there as soon as I can, Mother." He cut the connection, and concentrated on Lisa. "That was my mother. She's been arrested."

"For trying to murder my father? Good. Serves her right."

"If what she's just told me is true, then the whole thing is absurd. And if your father has accused her, it's more likely him living in cloud-cuckoo land... like so many others on this blasted estate."

For a moment, she trembled in white-faced fury. Then she sidestepped around him and stormed off. He recovered his composure and hurried after her.

Cursing his blind candour, he called out, "Lisa," as she hurriedly negotiated the crowds in the lounge bar.

"Chick with sense, eh, Ballcock?"

He glowered briefly into Lipton's amused eyes, then pushed his tormentor out of the way. "Just go away, you idiot." Turning once more, he rushed after her.

She was outside and hurrying to her car by the time he

caught up to her. "Lisa, where are you going?"

"Leeds."

"So am I. Wouldn't it make more sense for us to go together?"

She ignored his plea. "If I never see you again, Raymond Baldock, it will be too soon."

"Listen, Lisa, whatever has happened, I'm sure it's all a dreadful mix up, and I'm also sure we can sort it out better as a pair, rather than individuals."

A hand landed on his shoulder. "Who d'you think you're pushing about, Ballcock?"

Lipton, already drawing back his fist, spun Baldock, whose arms flailed as he turned. His half-clenched right fist caught Lipton a sideways, glancing blow on the nose. The half-drunk thug staggered back, blood pouring from his nose and down his white, Leeds United T-shirt, shock radiating from his eyes.

As surprised as his opponent, Baldock recovered first, and shouted, "For the last time, Lipton, get the hell away from me." He turned again to find Lisa looking at him with what he hoped was fresh respect. "Let's take my car," he suggested. "We can be there in fifteen minutes. I'll drop you at the hospital, go to the police station and join you at the hospital after I've sorted out my mother."

She stared angrily at him, even more angrily at Lipton, who was now using the T-shirt in an effort to stem the flow of blood from his nose. Finally, she stared at the Mercedes. "You're not going anywhere for a while."

He followed her gaze to find one of his wheels missing, the axle propped on house bricks.

Livid that he had not noticed the four-way flashers, which carried on working long after the tweet of the alarm cut out, Baldock raged at the night. "Oh, for heaven's sake… What is it about this estate—"

"You can't leave it there," Lisa said. "The other three wheels will be gone by the time you get back from Leeds."

"But I need to get to the police station to get my mother out."

Lisa gave it a moment's thought, after which she rounded on Lipton. "You. If there's one more wheel missing off his car, you get nailed for it."

Pressing the hem of his T-shirt to his nose again, his grotesque, hairy belly showing, Lipton protested his innocence. "It's nowt to do with me. I'm the injured party, here. He thumped me. And I've never touched his bloody car."

"What's that got to do with anything?" Lisa demanded. "Who do you think the filth will believe? You or me?"

"You cow."

"Call me that again and I'll bell the law now. Make sure his car still has four... er... three wheels tomorrow morning."

Lipton gave vent with an incomprehensible grunt, which Lisa apparently understood even if Baldock didn't.

"We'll take my car, Raymond," she said. "I'll drop you at the cop shop, then go on to the hospital."

Unwilling to argue further with any woman who could subdue the likes of Lipton, he climbed obediently into the passenger seat passenger seat of her red Fiesta. As he pulled the safety belt across his chest, she climbed behind the wheel, dragged her belt over and fired the engine.

"Where's your mother?"

"Kirkgate Police Station."

Pulling away from the pub, Lisa programmed the satnav.

"You need that to get you to Leeds?"

"I'm not absolutely sure where it is."

Baldock took over. "You drive, I'll navigate," he said, and took over the task. "Where is your father?"

"LGI, A & E and they're on the point of moving him to High Dependency." She reached the main road, and turned left. "I assume your mother has been arrested for assaulting him. That's what the hospital told me. Not that your mother was arrested, but that he's been assaulted."

"She didn't say," he admitted. "It's the nature of the charge that troubles me."

Lisa reached a large roundabout on the eastern extremities of the estate, and followed the signs for Bell Hill. "Nature of the charge? What do you mean?"

Baldock felt his ears colouring. "Attempted murder and, er, the kind of assault that would be in keeping with the film they went to see."

"Fifty Shades? Jesus, you mean she's crushed his—"

"I don't know," Baldock interrupted hastily. "Mother said she's been arrested for attempted murder and sexual assault. I mean, for God's sake, she's sixty-five years old. What kind of police officers does Leeds employ these days?"

Lisa did not answer and Baldock charitably assumed that similar thoughts were running through her mind.

She turned north towards the city. Baldock stared at the new-ish houses lining the road on either side; bog-standard, characterless two and three-bedroom, redbrick cheap and cheerful semis, a cut above council owned housing, and aimed at the upper strata of the working classes: the nouveau middle class. Once more, the innate snobbery of his thoughts did not occur to him. There were many similar estates in Norwich, but mercifully none that he was aware of in Wroxham.

"All this used to be open fields, didn't it?" he said, breaking into the monotonous thrum of the car's engine.

"Had a lot of fun in those fields when we were young."

Baldock knew what she meant. "I don't think I did."

"What else is new?"

Her words niggled once more. Baldock was not certain that he was the only virgin in his fresher year, but he always had the feeling that he was the only 18-year-old virgin from Midthorpe. The fields off the eastern side of the estate, behind the new comprehensive school were as notorious as Midthorpe Woods for primary sexual experiences, but at the time he had been more intent upon Shakespeare, Milton, Dickens, and Hardy. Sex, he had reasoned when suppressing the demands of his burgeoning libido, could wait until later.

While Lisa sped them towards the city centre, paying scant attention to the speed limits and the road humps designed to enforce those limits, Baldock concentrated on ringing the same wheel and tyre company which had rescued him earlier in the day.

"We've already done it, boss."

"Yes, I know you have. But some thieving swine has stolen it again. Is there any way you can secure those wheels so that no one but a professional can take them off?"

"We can alarm them," the tyre fitter told him.

"They're already alarmed. It doesn't seem to deter the thieves."

"We can secure them with locking nuts," the man offered.

"They have those, too, or didn't your man tell you so? It seems the thieves on Midthorpe can strip them out, and people are so used to alarms going off up here, they ignore the noise."

"In that case, all I can think is either swap them for bog-standard, boring wheels, and I'll swap my week in Torremolinos for a fortnight in Florida on the strength of the business you're bringing in."

After leaving him with instructions to replace the wheel and giving his credit card details, Baldock shut down the phone as Lisa turned towards the city centre and the lower end of Kirkgate market. A few minutes later, she dropped him at the police station.

"The moment I've sorted this out, I'll grab a taxi to the infirmary and meet you there," he promised.

Lisa tore off without answering, and he entered the station to be greeted by a surly desk constable, who, after listening to his garbled explanation, sent for Detective Inspector Dawn Kramer.

A forty-something redhead whose baggy eyes and general hangdog expression hinted at a long shift and no sign of an end to it, she greeted him with a brisk handshake. "I've read one or two of your novels. They're very accurate in depicting police work."

"I'm meticulous in my research and I've had great deal of help from the Norfolk Constabulary," he explained. "But right now, I'm concerned with the call from my mother. What on earth is going on?"

"She refused to talk to anyone until you arrived," Kramer

explained as she led him through the station to the back area.

"There's obviously some misunderstanding," Baldock insisted.

"We think so, too, but she will not speak to us without you being present. We offered to call a solicitor for her, but she said no. She wanted to call you. I asked if you had any legal training, and she admitted you didn't, but you'd know how to sort this out." Kramer stopped and faced him. "Before we go any further, Mr Baldock, I appreciate you're wealthy and you can probably call on some pretty influential people, but it won't change anything until your mother speaks to us."

Baldock resented the implication. "And in the meantime, you've thrown her into a cell, have you?"

"Good God, no. We wouldn't do that to a woman her age. She's in an interview room." Kramer marched on again and stopped outside the wooden door of Interview Room 2. "I have to tell you, Mr Baldock, that as we see them, the facts are clear cut. Your mother is guilty of sexual assault and attempted murder. Obviously, she hasn't been charged, but unless she talks to us, we will have no choice."

He nodded. "Let's see if I can get some sense out of her."

Kramer opened the door and ushered him in.

Sat at the table, with a uniformed woman constable in attendance, Janet was reading an old copy of *Yours* magazine. When they entered, she looked up and smiled on her son.

"Raymond. I'm so glad you're here." She turned to the uniformed constable. "Any chance of another cup of tea, Alison?"

"I'll arrange it, Janet."

Alison left, Baldock and Kramer took a seat opposite Janet, and Kramer took out a statement form.

Skimming through what had already been written there, she said, "While we're waiting for Alison to come back, I'll give you the facts, Mr Baldock. At eleven o'clock, we received a call from paramedics attending an emergency in room 104 of the Stannedge Hotel. They had been called out to man named Timothy Yeoman, who was having breathing difficulties. They found Mr Yeoman naked on the bed, struggling to breathe. He had a part-erection and the paramedics confirmed that his penis and testicles had been coated in candle wax. When questioned, Mrs Baldock, your mother, admitted that she had applied the wax, and also that she had given Mr Yeoman a Viagra substitute, which the paramedics say was the most likely cause of his respiratory problems. Mr Yeoman was taken to Leeds General Infirmary, where we understand he is currently in intensive care having ingested some kind of poison. Mrs Baldock was asked to explain, but she refused and was therefore arrested." Kramer looked up from the statement. "The rest, you already know."

Baldock's head was still spinning. He looked from his mother to Kramer and back again. Not one single word Kramer had said could be applied to his mother.

Crimson with embarrassment, he ventured, "I… er…"

Baldock was annoyed with himself. His mother sat across the table, a thin smile of expectation on her lips, a beam of motherly love and admiration in her eyes, and the only response he could come up with was, *I… er…*

Alison returned with tea for everyone, and when she had distributed three cups to the table, she took a seat at the back of the room.

Baldock took a swallow. It was ghastly. Too much sugar, and the milk was full-cream. He preferred skimmed. But if nothing else, it did invigorate him.

"Mother, what is going on here? You told me you were going to the cinema with the over-fifties, and then staying the night in a hotel with a friend."

"That's right. Tim was the friend."

The shock resounded through his system. His mother with another man? "But… but you never said. For God's sake, I was having dinner with Lisa, and she never said."

"That's because she doesn't know about us, Raymond." Janet narrowed disapproving eyes on him. "I don't see why my lovers should be any concern of yours. Tim is widowed, I'm divorced, and we got together."

"Lovers? You mean you have more than one?"

"Well, there have been other men since your father left,

but I only go out with them one at a time."

"But... but..."

"But what? Really, Raymond, for a supposed novelist, you're not very good with words, are you?"

"But... But, you're my *mother*."

"Yes dear, I am. I carried you and your brother for nine months." Putting down her cup, she patted her tummy. "How do you think you got in here? A stork? Immaculate Conception? Your father gave me a good seeing to, and you were the result."

Baldock almost spilled his tea and he noticed Kramer suppressing a smirk. "Mother, please."

Kramer sought to establish control over proceedings. "Mrs Baldock, now that your son's here, could you give us your account of what happened tonight?"

Janet sipped more tea. "We'd been to see Fifty Shades. Have you seen it, Inspector?"

"Er, no. I haven't."

"Wonderful film. Almost as good as the book. Very steamy. Very arousing. Tim and I knew we'd be horny when we'd seen it, but Raymond is staying with me at the moment, so Tim came up with the idea of staying at a hotel for the night. He's like that." Her eyes rested on her son again. "He treats me much better than your father ever did."

"That wouldn't be difficult," Baldock agreed. He was still reeling from the revelation of his mother feeling 'horny'.

"Now, Tim is diabetic," Janet went on. "He suffers from ED... erectile dysfunction." She stared at Baldock again. "He can't get it up."

He groaned as Kramer suppressed another smile. "I know what ED stands for, Mother."

"Yes, well, Tim usually takes Cialis. He finds it better than Viagra, which along with his diabetic pills, winds his stomach up a bit. Cialis is better all round. It stays in the body a lot longer than Viagra, and we tend to get more, er, excitement from a single pill, if you see what I mean?"

This time, Kramer could not suppress the smile, nor the laugh which went with it. "Please, go on, Mrs Baldock."

Her son would rather Janet shut up, but his mother was only just getting into her stride.

"Well the bloody fool forgot to bring the Cialis with him, didn't he? Typical man. Wouldn't know where to find his underpants if he didn't have a woman to show him. So I bought a substitute from a friend. Fiagara, it's called."

At last Baldock had something he could get a handle on, or not as the case may be. As long as it was a graphic description of his mother's insalubrious activities. "Fiagara?" he asked, and while Kramer made hurried notes, Janet answered.

"Well, the friend doesn't like to call it Viagra because it might be copyright or something."

"I think you mean a patent infringement," her son muttered.

"We're not really concerned with its name, Mrs Baldock," Kramer said. "Who is this friend?"

Janet shook her head. "I'm sorry. I'm no tittle-tattle. I can tell you that Tim has taken this Fiagara before and it's never bothered him, so whatever has made him ill, it isn't that."

"Do you have any other samples of this pill?" Kramer asked.

"No. I only bought the one. They're five pounds each, you know."

"Then I will have to insist that you tell me the name of the friend who supplied it."

"I'm, sorry. You can charge me with whatever you want, but I'm not telling you."

Kramer remained patient. "Mrs Baldock, if it should prove that this pill poisoned Mr Yeoman, you could be in serious trouble, and other men and women may be affected by it. At the very least you could be charged with obstructing the police in the course of their inquiries."

"I'll speak to her later," Baldock promised. "For now, Mother, tell us what happened in the room."

"Tim took the Fiagara before we left the Odeon. By the time we checked into the Stannedge, he was up for it. He took a shower while I melted the wax—"

"If I may ask, Mrs Baldock," Kramer interrupted. "Why did you need the wax?"

"I was taking a cast of his wedding tackle, dear."

Baldock almost fainted, and Kramer smiled again.

"Why?"

"To make a plaster model of it. One I can keep on the bedside cabinet."

"What?" Her son's colour returned with a deep blush. "Mother, most people keep a photograph on the bedside cabinet, not a…" He trailed off unable to find a suitable epithet.

"Well Tim has a photograph of me on his bedside cabinet. I'm topless. It was taken in Benidorm last year."

"Topless? Benidorm?"

"Yes, luv. It's in Spain. It's a good job we had our smartphones. Boots would never have developed some of those pictures."

Baldock tried to erase some of the mental images her words encouraged. "I don't know how much more of this I can take. Let's get back to the room at the Stannedge."

"Well, Tim had his shower, I got him up and then I began to put the wax on. It might have been a bit hot, because I heard him gasping, and then suddenly, he was in convulsions. He could hardly breathe. I got worried and called the desk downstairs. They sent for the paramedics, and the rest is history as Inspector Kramer said." Pleading eyes took them both in. "I didn't do anything deliberately. I love Tim, and there's no way I would ever hurt him. It was consexual."

"You mean consensual."

Janet shrugged. "Sexual, sensual. They mean the same, don't they?"

Feeling like an appendage to the debate, Baldock raised his eyebrows at Kramer.

The inspector was equally uncertain. "Our situation is complex. Based on what Mrs Baldock has told us, I'm not sure that any crime has been committed. We'll have to wait until we can speak to Mr Yeoman to confirm that. For now, my guess is it really was this…" Kramer consulted her notes,

"... this Fiagara which poisoned him. We won't know until we can get hold of a sample. There is the matter of applying hot wax to his privates, but considering he had an erection, it sounds as if it really was consensual. Right now, in refusing to give us the name of the person who supplied this Fiagara, your mother is certainly guilty of withholding evidence and obstructing the police in the course of their inquiries, but again I can't confirm the specific charges until we get a toxicology report from the infirmary. But I will ask again, Mrs Baldock, for the identity of the person who sold you the pill."

"And I'm sorry, but I won't tell you."

"Okay. I'm prepared to release you on police bail. You will be reported for refusing to cooperate with our inquiry and if toxicology confirms it is this pill, then you will be brought in for questioning again." Kramer addressed Baldock. "In the meantime, may I suggest, Mr Baldock, that you try to impress upon your mother the trouble she could be causing for herself, and the need to cooperate with our inquiry."

"Of course."

Kramer stood up and nodded to Alison that they should leave. "In that case you're free to go."

"There is one thing, Inspector," Janet asked as he got to her feet. "The wax casting. Is there any danger I could have it back?"

"I'm sorry, Mrs Baldock, but we have that item and it will be retained as evidence should any prosecution follow."

"Oh dear."

"What's wrong, Mother?"

"I don't think Tim would be too happy about having his todger handled by the jury."

Chapter Seven

Silence was the most notable thing about the short journey from the police station to the infirmary. Notwithstanding the presence of the taxi driver, Baldock was too irritated and confused to think of anything non-controversial to say to his mother, and Janet appeared too preoccupied to speak.

Only when Baldock paid the driver and they climbed out to look up at the concrete grey blocks of the famous Leeds General Infirmary, did Janet finally break the silence.

"Your grandma died here."

"Well, let's hope that's not an omen," Baldock said as he led her to the entrance.

He well-recalled his grandmother's death, fourteen years previously. He was a struggling journalist, eking out a living in North London, his brother had moved to Manchester, his lorry driver father was away on some long journey, and Janet was alone when her mother was taken ill. Hospitalised and having suffered a weak heart for most of her life, she gradually faded away over a period of about five days. Baldock arrived in Leeds, having scrounged some time off on the day of her death, and passed the last half hour of the old woman's life at her bedside. His brother, Keith, made the journey from Manchester to Leeds, but arrived ten minutes after her demise, but his father did not get back from Cornwall until two days later. As far as he could recall, Baldock, already disenchanted with his father, never spoke to the man again except under such circumstances as he was compelled.

Brief inquiries at the A & E reception, sent them to the High Dependency ward where the senior nurse refused them access.

"Mr Yeoman is very ill," she said, "and he's permitted only one person at his bedside. Right now, his daughter is with him."

Janet would have walked away, but Baldock's arrogance would not allow him to be bullied by a public servant, no matter how medically qualified she was. "Would you tell Ms Yeoman that Mrs Baldock is here, along with her son?"

The nurse was surprised. "You're Ms Yeoman's son?"

Baldock sighed. "I am Mr Baldock. Raymond Baldock. The novelist. I am Mrs Baldock's son, not Ms Yeoman's."

"I see. And you're a novelist. Tell me, is that germane to the issue? Is Mr Yeoman starring in one of your literary works?"

"No, but you might."

Her eyes brightened. "Really?"

"I'm thinking of a medical murder mystery, where the victim is an officious and obnoxious ward manager. Now would you please tell Ms Yeoman we are here?"

The nurse turned and marched stiffly away.

Less than a minute later, an angry Lisa burst through the double doors, her dagger eyes aimed straight at Janet. "What the hell have you done to my father?"

Baldock was about to intervene, but to his surprise, his mother stood her ground. "Nothing he didn't want me to do, Lisa. And I'll thank you to keep a civil tongue in your head when you speak to me."

Lisa was not remotely taken aback, nor put off her stride. "He's critical in there. You poisoned him."

"I did nothing of the kind. Stop behaving like a child, Lisa. Raymond and I came here because we're as concerned for your father as you are."

"If we could all calm down—"

"Would you be calm if it was your father in there?" Lisa interrupted Baldock.

He did not even think about it. "To be honest, if it was my father in that room, I don't think I'd even be here."

"Well, you never did have much time for him, did you?"

"Lisa." Baldock stressed her name. "I've spoken with the

police and I've listened to my mother's side of the story. I don't know what's happened to your father, but I do know it's the result of some dreadful mix-up, and not a deliberate attempt on his life. If we calm down, if you listen to what my mother has to say, and if the medics can tell us what has actually caused your father's condition, then we might make real progress."

Lisa's anger began to subside. "Let me have a word with the nurses." She turned back to the door and buzzed the intercom. A moment later, the ward manager emerged, Lisa had a brief and quiet word with her, after which the nurse, in louder tones, assured her that she would ring if there was any change. Lisa gestured to Baldock and Janet that they should retire to the café.

An all-night place, service at this hour was by vending machine only. One or two hospital employees, doctor and nurses, easily identified by their variously coloured overalls, occupied tables here and there, and other people, presumably visitors or those waiting for friends and family getting out of A & E, had also taken up tables.

While Janet and Lisa secured a table by windows overlooking the grandiose, twin spires of Leeds Civic Hall, Baldock secured coffee from a machine and joined them.

Taking a sip of coffee and grimacing, Janet said, "I don't really want to give you all the details, Lisa, but I have to or you won't understand. Raymond has heard them and he has trouble dealing with them."

"I find it all unbelievable," Baldock confirmed.

And with that, Janet launched into her tale.

Baldock switched off as much as he could and concentrated on Lisa, marvelling at the calm manner in which she listened and occasionally commented on Janet's explanation. It was stark contrast to his reaction. He had been not merely shocked, but utterly appalled at his mother's behaviour, and even more stunned by her candour.

It was the kind of tale he would expect from the general riff-raff living on Midthorpe, and it would cause him a good deal of irritation. 'Degenerate but entirely in keeping with the area' would be the phrase which sprang to mind. But to hear it from his own mother, to lump his mother, a woman he had always considered a cut above the rest of the Midthorpe hoi-polloi, was one shock too many to his system.

Lisa did not appear remotely interested in the games her father and Janet had been playing. Baldock wondered if she seethed with indignation inside; the way he had. If so, she did an excellent job of hiding it, and was more concerned with the revelation that Janet and Tim were 'an item' as his mother insisted on putting it.

"What I don't understand is why Dad never told me about you." Lisa was a good deal calmer having listened to Janet.

"I've often asked if he'd told you," Janet said, "and he always said he hadn't, but when I asked why, he would never give me a direct answer. I think he may have been worried that you'd think he was sullying – is that the right word, Raymond? – your mother's memory."

Before Baldock had a chance to confirm his mother's question, Lisa replied.

"He's talking a lot of rubbish. Mum has been dead for three years, and I've been telling Dad it's time he got out and about again, met other people, formed another relationship. He's only sixty-five. That's not old, Janet. You're the same age, and you're not old. I'm pleased for him, and I'm pleased for you." Her voice became a little sterner. "What I'm not pleased about is this fooling around with Viagra substitutes."

"We've used them before, Lisa."

Determined to nip the conversation in the bud before it could get into murky waters, Baldock began to protest. "Ladies, please—"

"Shut up, Raymond," Lisa ordered. She concentrated once more on Janet. "If Dad is prescribed Cialis, then Cialis, the genuine article, is what he should take. Wouldn't it make more sense for him to give you a pack of the pills so you can carry them in your handbag? That way, if he ever forgets to bring them, you still have some with you."

Janet's eyes lit up. "What a sensible idea. Just like women carrying condoms, isn't it? Compensating for a man's concentration on doing it rather than doing it safely."

"Mother please—"

"Shut up, Raymond." Janet smiled on Lisa. "I'll talk to Tim about it."

"If and when we get him back safely." Lisa's features darkened. "Something has poisoned him, and this Fiagara nonsense is prime suspect."

"He's taken it before," Janet insisted. "It never troubled him."

"Where did you get it, Janet?"

Baldock's mother retreated. "Ah, now, as I explained to Raymond and the police, that's a matter of some confidence, and I'm not prepared to say. Besides, as I've just said, Tim has taken this before, but it's never been any trouble."

A broody silence followed and they all drank the coffee.

"Lisa?" Janet sounded tentative. "Would you mind if I sat with your father for a few minutes?"

"They have him sedated, Janet. He can't communicate."

"I know. I'd just like to be with him for a little while."

Lisa nodded and dug out her phone. "I'll speak to the ward manager."

While she rang the ward, Baldock saw an opportunity.

"One condition, Mother. Who sold you this Fiagara?"

Finishing off her coffee, Janet shook her head. "No deal."

"Then I'll tell the ward manager you're currently suffering an infection and you shouldn't be allowed anywhere near him."

"Raymond—"

"Mother, think about this. It's not for Tim's sake. He's taken this pill, and like Lisa, I believe that it's the cause of his problems. It could just be a bad batch, but how many other men will take the pill and suffer the same consequences? And how many of them are likely to end up here, or worse, in the mortuary? We're not police, we can't arrest your supplier, but someone has to stop him."

Across the table, Lisa shut down her phone and watched with interest and he went on.

"This silly notion of tell no tales is entirely fitting for most of the scroats who live on Midthorpe, but it doesn't apply to real life, Mother. This supplier needs to be stopped before he actually kills someone."

"He could go to prison, Raymond."

"And if he's selling poison, he deserves to."

For the first time since he arrived on Midthorpe earlier in the day, Baldock felt himself to be in complete control of events.

"His name, Mother, or you don't get to see Tim."

"Ooh, you are cruel to your mother."

"Only with the intention of being kind, Janet," Lisa assured her. "Tell us who sold you the Fiagara. I'll do what I can to ensure he's treated fairly."

"If you're going to the police, I'll not tell you."

"Mother."

"Oh, all right." Janet hesitated a moment. "Michael Shipston."

Both Lisa and Baldock were wide-eyed, but for different reasons.

"Shippy? He still lives on Midthorpe?" Baldock demanded.

"More to the point, what was he doing with the over-fifties club? He's younger than both of us." Lisa's finger pointed to Baldock and herself in turn, identifying the 'us'.

"He drove the minibus to town. You know he owns one, Lisa."

"Yes. I also know he's not licenced to carry passengers and he probably wasn't insured."

"No. But he was cheap." Janet took all three plastic cups and stacked them up. "We were half way to Leeds when your dad realised he'd forgotten to bring the Cialis. We didn't have time to go back for it, so when we got to the hotel, I had a quick word with Shippy and he sold me a pill. I told you. I've bought them from him before, and he wouldn't sell me poison."

"He was always hooky," Baldock said. "Not that anyone on Midthorpe would care."

"Raymond, will you forget your downer on Midthorpe for

a minute?" Lisa scolded him. "Janet, does Shippy make them himself?"

"I shouldn't think so, dear. He's hard pressed to make a cheese sandwich never mind pills."

"Then we need to know where he got them." Baldock stood. "So, if we're ready…"

The two women showed no inclination to go anywhere.

"I want to see Tim," Janet declared.

"The nurse is expecting you," Lisa confirmed before sending Baldock a thin smile. "I can't go anywhere. Not until I know he's out of danger. And anyway, Raymond, who are you going to find to question at this time of the morning?"

Baldock sat down again as Janet left them.

A long silence followed. Baldock stared gloomily though the windows and out at the night, Lisa gazed at her hands surrounding her near empty cup. He struggled to find something to say and finding nothing, remained silent. The entire evening had been a disaster, from the moment they settled at their table in The Midden, and he knew exactly where the blame lay: Midthorpe.

"I, er, I'm sorry, Raymond. The way I reacted earlier."

Her words, cutting into the silence startled him. Lisa treated him to a bleak smile.

Baldock looked at his watch. Almost one a.m. "I'll get us fresh coffee." He crossed to the machine and returned a few moments later with two cups.

Lisa sipped the froth from hers. "I notice you have cash on you."

He grunted humourlessly. "After Haigh's this morning, I called at the ATM. I had to pay you what I owed you, if you recall." He too sipped the tasteless beverage. "Look… Your behaviour earlier. It doesn't matter. I realise you were upset and just sounding off. I said at the time there'd been a mix-up, but your greater concern was your father's welfare. I understand that. I felt the same about my mother."

"But you didn't blame my dad."

"I couldn't. Your remarks in The Midden made no sense because I didn't know about your dad and my mum at the time." His face fell. "I wish I didn't know about them now."

"You disapprove?"

It was as much a statement as a question and it caused Baldock to search his feelings.

"No. Not disapprove. I'm surprised, I think. Surprised that she never said anything. It's getting on for four years since Dad walked out on Mum. She had a bad time of it. All those years married, and he ups sticks to live with that tart who worked in the bookies at the top of Midthorpe Avenue. I could have bloody killed him for it. So I don't blame her for finding someone else." He raised his eyebrows at Lisa. "How do you feel about it?"

"The same as you. Mum died three years ago, and Dad took it badly. The cancer had eaten away most of her insides by the time she passed away, and he watched her waste away to nothing, powerless to do anything other than be there and help control her pain. And it's not the dead who suffer you know. They're beyond any pain. It's the living. Those left behind. For me, it was a relief when it was all over, but it tore him to pieces. I was there. I stood by him, did what I could for him, but he pined and pined for her, got mad with himself because he couldn't do anything for her. He was racked with guilt. A natural stage of grief. Then he withdrew into himself. I think that's when the diabetes really kicked in."

Tears sparked the corners of her eyes, and she took a moment and another slug of coffee to compose herself. Baldock wanted to reach across the table and take her hand, show that he understood, but his natural reticence stopped him.

"He needed to get out," she went on. "He needed to be with people, he needed another woman in his life. And quite honestly, it was always going to be a Midthorpe woman, and if he had to choose, he couldn't have chosen better than Janet Baldock. They'll be better than good for each other. My dad is a gentleman, your mother is a party animal. What better combination could you have?"

"Yes, well, I suppose I go along with all you're saying, but…"

Lisa waited a few seconds before prompting him. "But?"

"I could have done without Mother giving me the nitty-gritty."

Lisa threw back her head and laughed, sending a wave of near-relief through him.

"Sex, sex, sex. Raymond, it's a reasonable assumption that when two people get together, they will have sex."

He felt his ears colouring again. "I know that. I'm simply saying I didn't need it spelling out in such minute detail."

"And if it hadn't been for what happened to my dad, if it hadn't been for the police rushing your mother to the police station, you wouldn't have had it spelled out. None of us would. I'm sure Janet would have preferred to keep it between her and Dad, and I'm certain Dad wouldn't speak to me about it."

Baldock was not so sure and said so. "She was quite proud of it."

"Proud of embarrassing you, you mean."

"No, I don't know what you mean."

"Oh come on, Raymond. You're a stuffed shirt, aren't you? You always were. I said as much earlier this evening. People think you're the way you are because you went to Cambridge, but I remember when we were kids, and you were always the same. Fuddy-duddy."

"I refute that," he argued. "I simply believe there are standards and they should be maintained, and *seen* to be maintained."

"The trouble is your standards belong back in the nineteenth century. Your mother was a teenager in the sixties, like my dad. Free spirits. They behave as they behave and bugger the rest of the world."

"Which is all well and good, but does it need to be discussed with your son... or daughter? And if it does, do you really need to relish it like Mother does?"

"Yes. If you see in your son – or daughter – someone who is disturbed by your antics." Lisa spread her hands. "Shock treatment. Let your brats know that you're human with its fripperies and frailties."

Baldock harrumphed. "Those fripperies and frailties have got them both into trouble. What are we going to do about getting them out of it?"

"You're the one who writes detective stories. You tell me. Do you know anything about how the police really work?"

"Quite a lot," he admitted. "The success of the Headingley novels has meant I've been able to spend time with the police. I've sat in with patrols, attended CID briefings, and I've spoken to any number of officers from beat bobbies to senior detectives and the upper echelons."

"So where will this Inspector Kramer go from here?"

Relieved to be on firmer ground, Baldock considered the question, his brow knitted into deep furrows. "First she needs to establish that some crime has been committed, and my mother's insistence that the, er, incidents were consensual throws some doubt on that. Kramer has said as much, and she will need to speak to your father."

"That's not going to be possible for at least twenty-four hours," Lisa said.

"And until then, my mother remains under suspicion. However, even if you father clears my mother, there is the issue of what's actually caused the problem." He fixed Lisa's gaze with his. "Do we both agree that the most likely cause is this Fiagara?"

She nodded. "Unless there was something in one of their meals, but if so, why didn't it affect your mother?"

"Kramer will wait for toxicology reports before she does anything. If it should prove to be the Fiagara – what an absolutely silly name for this thing – then she will insist that my mother identifies her supplier. If mother refuses, and she probably will, then she becomes guilty of withholding evidence, possibly obstructing the police in the course of the duties. She could face a substantial fine, probation, even prison, and I can't allow that."

"So what are you going to do? You'll appreciate, Raymond, that this is all concern for your mother, and I can understand that. But I have a different agenda. Seeing my dad out of here and well again."

"Yes. Of course. But as I said to Mother earlier, we should stop this stuff spreading any further. If it's hit your dad like that, how many other men will it bring down? I think we should tell Kramer what we've learned."

"About Shippy?"

Baldock nodded.

"Why not confront him?" Lisa asked.

"Well, er… I think it's better if the police—"

"Rules and standards again, Raymond?" Lisa leaned forward and jabbed her finger into the table. "Listen to me. This man poisoned my father and he should rightly be handed over to the cops. But first, he's going to get more than a piece of my mind. You suit yourself, Raymond, but once they give me the all-clear here, I'll be going to see Michael Shipston."

Chapter Eight

Baldock's eyes flickered open at just before ten on Saturday morning, and he immediately wanted to go back to sleep.

There had been a slight improvement in Tim's condition, but the hospital did not expect him to make further progress overnight, and since he was out of danger and unlikely to deteriorate, they came home. Lisa dropped them off at his mother's house just before three-thirty in the morning.

After a cup of tea and a brief chat with his mother, Baldock climbed into bed a little after four and was asleep in minutes.

Now, less than six hours later, he was awake again, reminding himself of just how gruelling Friday had been. He'd got up at five, driven from Norwich to Leeds, spent the day here and there on Midthorpe, had dinner with Lisa, fooled around with his car wheels, and to top it all, there'd been the aftermath of his mother's little adventure. All up it came to twenty-one, non-stop hours, after which, less than six hours sleep did little to ease his overall fatigue.

Crossing the landing to the bathroom, he heard muttered voices from downstairs. His mother on the telephone, he guessed. She was probably disseminating the previous night's 'excitement' to her friends.

Soaking under a hot shower, he slipped into his memory and shuddered. Exciting was the last word he would choose. Embarrassing for the most part, and infuriating. Why couldn't people learn to behave themselves? That same woman, whom he truly loved, had drilled into him the need to behave when he was a child, and stressed it time and again when he was a teenager, before finally, tearfully ramming home the message when he left Cambridge, and he had taken it on board. He did behave. His manners and conduct were impeccable, and if he did get irritated, it was with the feckless, workshy benefit scroungers; people like Midthorpers. Them and the minions of this world who insisted upon laying down their petty rules and regulations as if they were the be-all and end-all. People like young Ivan Haigh, who refused to move into the 21st century.

And now, here was his mother indulging in bedtime romps with a fellow senior citizen like a couple straight out of an internet porn movie. Baldock would not have minded so much if Tim Yeoman had been taken ill in the cinema or restaurant. He wouldn't have been so troubled if they'd been to see another movie. But Fifty Shades followed by an unseemly carry on at a cheap hotel…

"Your mother seems determined to shag my father to death," Lisa had commented in the café while they waited for Janet to rejoin them.

"Curious. I was just about to say the same to you,." He smiled. "Without the Anglo-Saxon, of course."

He towelled off and stood before the bathroom mirror, shaving, the rugged features, sharp, blue eyes gazing back at him and asking questions.

Like most things in life, his attitude to sex was quite conservative. He remained doggedly unmarried, preferring to live alone, but he acknowledged his libido and its demands upon him. On those occasions when he did entertain a lady, it was straightforward, missionary position, eyes shut, with the lights out… as it should be.

How could his mother…

A knock on the door distracted him. "Are you in there, Raymond? Only I need the toilet."

"One minute, Mother."

He swilled off in cold water, and turned to leave. At the last second, he remembered he was naked, and wrapped a bath towel round his waist. At the age of thirty-six, it was not the done thing to be seen in the altogether in front of one's mother.

He stepped out of the bathroom and with a nod of greeting

to Janet, crossed to his bedroom, while she hurried into the smallest room. By the time he had dressed in a pair of Levi jeans, a close-fitting Tommy Hilfiger T-shirt and Nike trainers, Janet was coming out of the lavatory.

"I'll cook you some breakfast, but then I have to go down to the infirmary. Tim's much better. He should be able to speak to me, and he may be coming home this afternoon."

"Have you told Lisa?" Baldock asked, following her down the stairs.

"She told me. I was just on the phone to her. I think she's a bit miffed that Tim asked for me, not her, but she's going to see him this afternoon... if he's still in hospital."

Emerging into the kitchen, Baldock looked out through the window at his Mercedes, now with all four wheels present and parked where he had asked the tyre company to leave it.

Putting aside thoughts of the cost of two new wheels, he asked, "Would you like me to run you to the infirmary?"

"No. It doesn't cost me anything. I have my bus pass." Spreading rashers of bacon on the grill tray, she slid it into the cooker and checked the setting. "Besides, did I hear you making arrangements to meet Lisa this morning?"

Baldock had not forgotten, but he turned from the window putting on the face of a man who had just been reminded of an appointment.

"What? Lisa? I... oh, yes. Of course. We're, er, we're going to see Shippy."

"Now Raymond—"

"I'm not going to let you carry the can for this, Mother. We won't be saying anything to police – yet – but we need to confront him, let him know what damage he's caused."

"But you don't know that it was the Fiagara," Janet protested. "I told you, Tim's used it before with no ill effects."

"Can you think of anything else?" Baldock demanded. "Food in the restaurant?"

"A fast food joint attached to the cinema. If it was there, there'll be plenty more cases."

"Drinks in the bar, then?"

"We didn't have any drink. It gives Tim the brewer's droop."

"I do wish you wouldn't be so blasé about these things." Baldock tutted his disapproval. "Still, it does show you that Fiagara is the only possible culprit."

"I won't—"

He cut her off once more. "Mother, I am not going to stand by and watch you hauled into court for withholding evidence. And Lisa isn't willing to stand back and see her father floored like this without making someone answer for it. She and I will be seeing Shippy in an effort to get him to own up."

Janet set the table and pointed to a chair. "Sit down. Breakfast will be five minutes."

***

As far as Baldock's memory served, Michael Shipston had lived his whole life on Nimmons Mount, a short cul-de-sac on the far, west side of the estate. It puzzled him, then, when Lisa asked him to meet her outside a house on Nimmons Lane.

The Lane ran East to West on the south side of the old school, from Midthorpe Avenue to Nimmons Crescent, one of those longer roads which between them encircled the estate. A small parade of shops sat on the Lane overlooking the school playing field, and Baldock had always believed the traders made huge profits from the pockets of children going to and from Midthorpe Primary and Secondary.

Beyond the shops was a single row of houses, less than two dozen in number dotted between streets running off the Lane, and it was outside one of these that he found Lisa's car parked.

She climbed out of her Fiesta as he pulled in behind her. Dressed in a pair of tight jeans and close-fitting top, her dark hair pulled back in a ponytail, she excited his near-dormant libido, and he hoped his appearance, all expensive, brand name clothing, would meet with her approval as much as hers met his.

To his disappointment, she did not comment upon his attire, but she did explain why they were meeting here.

"Kirsty Shipston," she said waving at the house. "She's Shippy's wife and technically, they're separated pending a divorce. The records say he lives with his mother on Nimmons Mount, but in fact, he still lives with Kirsty and spends most of his time here."

"Odd arrangement for a divorcing couple," Baldock commented following Lisa up the path to the front door.

"Not when you're both out of work and claiming benefits. It's more profitable to live alone."

"But... but..." Steam was coming out of Baldock's ears. "That's fraud."

"Welcome back to Midthorpe, Raymond." Lisa rattled the doorknocker. "Tell me, have you had the opportunity to live in the real world since you became a successful novelist?"

"I work hard for my living, Lisa, and I don't like to see my taxes thrown to people like these who are too lazy to work."

"Or too busy trying to bring up their children. And for your information, Shippy does work. It's fiddle, obviously, but he does do a bit." The door opened and Lisa smiled down on a child of about five. "Hi, Kylie. Is your dad in?"

The child shook her head.

"All right then, can we see your mum?"

Kylie closed the door.

"There are child care options," Baldock argued while they waited.

"They cost a fortune and most of the jobs round here wouldn't pay enough to cover the cost of care for one child, never mind five. Shippy does odds and sods of work to supplement his dole money. Like running his taxi service." She frowned again. "Don't look like that, Raymond. Bringing up children is expensive."

"Then they shouldn't have had so many. Or don't they believe in contraception either?"

"Even rubbers cost a fortune when you're on pocket money wages. It's called the poverty trap. People like you with all your millions, or the politicians spouting their trite excuses or laying off the blame for cock-ups, might not believe it exists, but it does. I know. I deal with its ramifications every day."

"I'm aware of all that, but..." He trailed off as the door opened and Kirsty Shipston appeared.

Aged about thirty-five, broad in hip and tummy, her tangle of copper-coloured hair was spread around her chubby face in a haphazard manner which many of the women in Baldock's circle of acquaintances would probably pay a fortune to duplicate. In Kirsty's case, judging from the empty eyes, it appeared to be natural.

"Hi, Kirsty," Lisa greeted. "We'd like a word with Mick, if possible. Is he out working?"

"Nope."

Lisa let out an exasperated breath. "Come on, Kirsty, you know me. I'm not from the Benefits people. Is he grafting?"

"Nope. He's in dry dock."

Baldock's brain thundered back twenty years and promptly translated the slang. "Hospital?"

"Yep."

Lisa's brow furrowed. "What's wrong with him?"

"Emergency last night. Couldn't breathe. Too many fags, I reckon, but he were, like, purple when I called t'ambulance."

"So what's wrong with him?" Baldock asked.

"I told you. He couldn't breathe."

Now it was Baldock's turned to sigh. "What caused his breathlessness? And don't tell me too many cigarettes."

"How the bloody hell should I know?"

"They didn't tell you at the hospital?" Lisa asked.

"Didn't go, did I? Couldn't. Had to look after the kids."

Baldock considered this. "Couldn't you have got someone to look after them for you?"

"Nope. My ma was out on the razz and his ma's losing her marbles."

"Your father, then?"

Kirsty snorted. "Even my old lady doesn't know who he is never mind me."

Frustration began to get the better of Baldock. "What about his father?"

"He's in Ireland."

"What's he doing over there?"

"Ten years, I think."

Baldock's jaw dropped and Kirsty went on to explain.

"He got nicked trying to get a container load of illegal immos through the port at Dublin. I wouldn't care but he'd driven right across England with 'em and no one batted an eyelid all the way from Hull to Holyhead."

"I don't believe I'm hearing this," Baldock muttered.

"And I don't believe it's any of our business," Lisa told him. "Listen, Kirsty, did Mick swallow any pills last night?"

For the first time, Kirsty looked uncomfortable. "Well, I don't... what do you wanna know for?"

"Did he swallow a pill called Fiagara? A Viagra substitute."

Kirsty went fully on the defensive. "It's not his fault, you know. The droop. What with him scratching and scraping for work an'all. I mean he took all them old fogies to t'pictures last night, and when he got home with a bit of brass in his pockets, well, I were feeling a bit... you know."

"Frisky?"

"Yeah. Right. I mean, it's not illegal is it? Only knowing this government—"

Baldock cut in on her. "He swallowed the Fiagara so he could, er, satisfy your needs?"

"Yes? And what's wrong with that?"

"Nothing," Lisa reassured her. "Where is he, Kirsty?"

"I told you. He's in t'hospital."

"Which one?"

Kirsty shrugged "Search me. I'll know when he rings me, won't I?"

"And how do you hope he'll do that if he can't talk?" Baldock demanded logically.

"He can text, can't he?" A loud crash from inside the house forced Kirsty to turn her head and shout, "I'll paste someone in a minute." She turned back to Baldock and Lisa.

"Look, I'll have to go. If you find him, will you tell him we need some milk on his way home?"

Lisa stayed her. "Just a minute, Kirsty. Does Shippy have any more of these pills in the house?"

Again Kirsty looked doubtful. "Well, I, er..."

Frustration began to get the better of Baldock. "Mrs Shipston, the reason Shippy is in hospital is the Fiagara. It poisoned him. It also poisoned Lisa's father."

Lisa tutted. "I don't think my dad would be too pleased about you letting half the estate know that he uses Viagra or substitutes."

"This young woman isn't half the estate, and—"

"It's as good as," Lisa interrupted.

Baldock was about to cut in on Lisa, but Kirsty got there first.

"Hey. I don't spread tales. I haven't got a big mouth."

"Shippy says different."

"How would he know? He hasn't got enough to fill a woman's mouth."

Lisa blushed. "I didn't mean it like that."

It was Kirsty's turn to turn on the acid, but Baldock intervened.

"Ladies, please. This is getting us nowhere. Kirsty, these pills have poisoned Shippy. Do you know who else he sells them to?"

Kirsty shrugged. "He's mentioned John Taplin and Malcolm Norris in the past. Dunno if he was flogging 'em any last night, though."

"We'll go see them," Lisa said. "Now, does Shippy have any Fiagara in the house?"

"Hang on a minute."

Clearly angry, Kirsty disappeared into the house. Baldock and Lisa waited and listened to the various bumps and bangs coming from within. A child began to cry, Kirsty screamed invective at another one or possibly more children, and the whole lot came to a cacophonous end with a huge crash of crockery and a scream of, "Now look what you've done. I'll bleeding kill you."

At length, Kirsty reappeared and slapped a single pill in Lisa's hand. The size of a 5p coin, the correct shade of blue with a single letter 'F' imprinted in the centre, it was folded amateurishly into a small piece of bubble wrap.

As Lisa took the pill, Kirsty held out her hand. "Fiver."

"What?" Baldock complained. "You expect us to pay for it?"

"That's how much Mick charges for it."

"Yes, but these are illegal drugs."

"So who gives a flying one? He's paid good money for it. I'm not letting it go without you pay for it."

Baldock dug out his phone. "Let's see what the police have to say about this, eh?"

Lisa stopped him. "It doesn't matter, Raymond. Give her a fiver. I'll pay you back."

"Yes, but this stuff is—"

"Just give her a fiver, Raymond, and let's go."

Grumbling, Baldock handed over the five pound note, and Kirsty turned into the house and closed the door behind her.

"So how are we going to find Shippy?" Lisa asked as they walked back to their cars.

"There are only two places, aren't there? The infirmary or St James's. We could try the infirmary and if we've no luck there, we could go to Jimmy's."

"Better yet, we could let Inspector Kramer know about it." Lisa chewed her lip. "We should tell her anyway. Two cases, both linked to Fiagara. She needs to get on the track of that pill."

"I agree." Baldock injected just enough inflection to let Lisa know he had reservations.

"You agree, but?"

"The police will be notoriously slow and precise on this, Lisa. I've no doubts they'll track Shippy down, and if he's on the mend, they'll talk to your dad, although there's not much point because we've tracked the source back from him. The police will wait for Shippy to come round before moving the investigation on any further, and even then it'll only happen if Shippy is willing to talk."

"Which, given his track record, is unlikely."

"We don't even know how far down the chain he is," Baldock pointed out, and the notion prompted another. "You don't think he's making the stuff, do you?"

"Shippy?" Lisa barked a laugh. "Never in a million years. I can see him as a dealer, but he doesn't have the wit to make this kind of stuff. You'd need a laboratory and a pill press. A big one if you want to shift the stuff in any quantity."

"Not necessarily; he could be buying them in over the web."

"And what do you think he'd be using for money, Raymond? You've seen how he and Kirsty are living, and these foreign suppliers tend not to offer a line of credit. Besides, it's easy enough to check. All you have to do is Google it." She shook her head and her ponytail wafted attractively from side to side. "No, you called it right. Shippy is only a link in the chain and we don't know how far along that chain he is." Lisa unlocked her car. "Listen, Raymond, I have to be at the hospital for two. I want to see my dad. And before then we have to check on John Taplin and Malcolm Norris. Then, we could squeeze in a bite of lunch if you fancied it. My treat. You paid last night."

"Nonsense. You may be well paid for your work, but I still earn more than you. Where? The Midden again?"

"It's where I usually go. One condition, though."

"Lisa, I will not allow you to pay."

"No. It's not that. If you want to pay, fine. It saves me a bob or two, and if that doesn't prove I'm a genuine Midthorper, I don't know what will. Will you agree to let me call Inspector Kramer and let her know about Shippy? At least they should be able to track him down."

He nodded and aimed the remote at his car to kill the alarm. "I'll follow you to Taplin's and Norris's."

Chapter Nine

"We have some news, Mr Yeoman, Mrs... er... Yeoman?"

Janet had been at Tim's bedside for almost half an hour when Dr Maclaren, identified by his badge as a junior medic, appeared.

Tim had recovered markedly overnight. He no longer needed help with his breathing, his colour was good, and if he appeared tired and drawn, it had more to do with lack of genuine sleep and a hangover from the drugs he had been given than any adverse effects of the previous night. But he found it difficult to speak, as a result of which, Janet did most of the talking bringing him up to date on overnight events between Lisa, herself and her son. Holding her hand, Tim had confined himself to occasional hoarse chuckles, and gestures, gripping her hand a little tighter or releasing his grip and patting her hand as sign of understanding and/or approval.

On Maclaren's query regarding her relationship, she was hesitant. "It's Mrs Baldock, actually. I'm Tim's, er, partner."

"Oh." The doctor, dressed in standard, pale green, NHS overalls, stethoscope hanging loosely over his neck as if it were some kind of badge of authority, appeared slightly confused and consulted his notes. "We have Mr Yeoman's next of kin as his daughter, Lisa."

"Lisa won't be here until this afternoon," Janet replied.

"Just tell us, Doc," Tim croaked. "Whatever you have to say, Janet is allowed to hear it."

Maclaren shrugged. "Okay. We've identified the poison. Household drain cleaner."

Answering for Tim, Janet tried to hide her surprise. "Oh. Well, that is odd. We weren't at home when the incident occurred."

"So I understand." Maclaren consulted Tim's notes once again. "Now, according to the reports, Mr Yeoman had swallowed some kind of Viagra substitute."

Tim nodded and Janet confirmed verbally.

"That's right. Fiagara. I bought it from a mutual friend. It's perfectly safe. He's taken it before."

Maclaren smiled indulgently, and shook his head. "Judging from our analysis of his stomach contents, I'd have doubts about that. The pill appears to have no active ingredient, but it is the source of the drain cleaner."

Janet was not about to be contradicted by a young man who probably had no need of any libidinous enhancement, genuine or otherwise. "That's not possible. I just told you, he's taken it before with no ill effects."

Maclaren perched himself on the edge of Tim's bed. "Mr Yeoman, Mrs Baldock, the problem with buying these alleged substitutes is you never know what they contain. The pills you've taken in the past may have been safe, although they won't have had any effect, but what you have this time is the product of a bad batch. These small laboratories don't operate to the same standards of hygiene as pharmaceutical companies. Don't ask me how drain cleaner got in there, but it did. Fortunately—"

Janet interrupted. "Excuse me, Doctor, but no effect? They've helped Tim get it up in the past."

Tim tried to protest, and Janet hastened to reassure him.

"I know we're talking as if you're not here, Tim, but you need to rest your voice and someone has to tell the doctor the tale. Now be a love, and shut up." She faced Maclaren again. "These pills work."

Maclaren delivered a benign smile; the kind usually reserved for simpletons. "May I ask how serious an issue is Mr Yeoman's ED?"

"At our time of life, it's serious a few times a month."

"It's common in diabetic men." Again Maclaren flipped through the notes. "His normal prescription is Tadalafil. Yes?"

"No. Cialis."

"Tadalafil is Cialis, Mrs Baldock."

"Oh. Right."

"And how long has Mr Yeoman been taking Tada... Cialis?"

"Certainly for the last year or more."

"Longer than that, Doc," Tim rasped.

"It seems to me then, that this Fiagara, used as a substitute or a top up, acts only as a placebo. Trust me, our analysis is accurate. Fiagara has no active ingredients... well, in this case, it has one active ingredient: sodium hydroxide, which is found in household drain cleaner. The rest of the pill was made up of sugar, chalk, colouring and ordinary bread dough."

Janet felt deflated. "I see. And how bad is the damage? To Tim, I mean?"

"Fortunately, it's not serious." Maclaren beamed on Tim. "You've been lucky, sir. You'll have a sore throat for a few days, and you may find you have the odd respiratory episodes, but you should be fine in a week."

"When can he come home?" Janet asked.

Maclaren laughed. "How quickly can you get dressed, Mr Yeoman?"

Tim sat up. "Get out of here, both of you, and let me get changed," he ordered in a barely audible whisper.

Janet stood up. "I'll call Lisa and Raymond. One of them can come and pick us up."

She and the doctor came away from the bedside, Maclaren drawing the screens so Tim could dress.

"Are you cohabiting, Mrs Baldock?" Maclaren asked as they ambled along the ward. "Living together?"

"Not yet," she replied. "In the near future, perhaps."

"He's going to need someone nearby for a few days. Just in case there are any respiratory complications. I'll write up a prescription for an inhaler. Salbutamol. One puff when he needs it, and he should see his GP in about a week. Just to check everything is all right."

They stopped at the nurses' station, where Maclaren began to write out the prescription. "Plenty of liquids. They'll help ease the burning in his throat. Ordinary painkillers should deal with any discomfort, and his system will naturally flush out the toxins. Oh, and one other thing, Mrs Baldock. Go easy on the candle wax for the time being."

Janet blushed. "You must think we're awfully perverted."

"I don't judge. I merely repair the damage."

They parted company and Janet continued out into the corridor. She switched on her phone and called Lisa. After a few minutes of debate, they agreed to come down in Baldock's Mercedes on the reasonable grounds that it would be less likely to lose wheels while he was actually driving it. By the time Janet had concluded the call, Tim was making his way out to the corridor.

From the first floor, they made their way down to the cafeteria, where Janet secured a much-needed cup of tea, and Tim settled for still water, whispering that it was kinder to his throat.

"I think you'd better stay with me for a few days," Janet said as she returned and settled in alongside him.

"What about Raymond?" Tim's voice was a hoarse, barely audible croak.

"Well, after last night, he knows everything, so he'll just have to put up with it, won't he? Besides, he's going home on Monday."

"What a..." Tim trailed off and swallowed water. Reaching into his pocket, he took out a small diary and pen and scribbled, *Hurts to talk. What a complete cock up.*

"From my point of view, that's the last thing it was," Janet tittered. "But we're not out of it yet, Tim. The police think I did this deliberately, so they'll want to talk to you. And Raymond and Lisa have been nagging me to tell the police about Michael Shipston. In fact, I'll bet they've already told that Inspector Kramer."

Someone has to, Tim scrawled. *We don't know how many more he sold or who he sold them to.*

***

Lisa and Baldock had not managed to get to The Midden when Janet rang asking them to come and collect her and Tim.

They had spoken to John Taplin's wife and Malcolm Norris's partner, and both had confirmed that their other halves were hospitalised with similar symptoms to Tim. Baldock called Inspector Kramer, gave all the details and received a promise that she and her team would get onto the matter, after which he and Lisa made for The Midden. It was as they arrived that Janet rang, and their lunch plans were aborted. Instead, Lisa left her car outside the pub and they travelled to Leeds in Baldock's Mercedes.

"You're not worried about leaving your car there?" Baldock had asked as they drove away. "I've had two wheels taken in the last twenty-four hours."

"Everyone knows it's my car, and no one will put so much as a dirty fingerprint on it never mind nick the wheels. Besides, there's no market for boring Ford wheels. Not like there is for the Mercedes brand alloys."

By one o'clock, Janet and Tim were in the rear seat of Baldock's luxury car, on their way back to Midthorpe and Lisa brought them up to date from the front passenger seat.

Janet was appalled when she heard that Shipston himself had been hospitalised. "I shouldn't have thought a man of his age needed any help in that department."

"Poetic justice," Tim croaked.

With one eye on the busy, Saturday afternoon traffic, Baldock agreed. "That's how I see it, but there is the problem of how many more of these poisons he's sold, and who did he sell them to?"

"Told you," Tim commented barely loud enough for the front passengers to hear.

Janet ignored him. "And I suppose you've told Inspector Kramer."

"We have, Mother," Baldock admitted. "We had to. We don't even know where the ambulance took Shippy. I just said, didn't I, that if there are any more of these pills out there, they need to be tracked down and disposed of."

"Well, if Shippy recovers as quickly as Tim did, you'll be able to ask him, won't you?"

"It's not up to me to ask anyone, Mother. I write detective fiction, but I'm not a detective. Let's leave it to Inspector Kramer and her people."

Silence fell as they turned off the main road and headed towards Midthorpe.

"Raymond," Janet ventured, "Tim will be staying at my house until he's well."

"That's no problem, Mother. I'll book into a hotel."

"Oh, you don't have to—"

"Don't do that," Lisa interrupted as Janet tried to protest. "Stay with me. I have room."

Baldock's pulse increased. He concentrated on his driving as he replied. "That's kind of you, but I don't want to be a burden."

"Don't be daft. Besides, it will be nice for me to have some company for a change." Lisa sounded as if she were looking forward to it.

"Only if you're sure."

"Definite."

"I'll need to collect a few things from Mother's first."

"Naturally," Lisa agreed. "And I don't know about you, but I could do with that bite to eat we never got."

"As soon as we drop my mother and your father off."

***

They took a late lunch in the Midthorpe Café, at the top of Midthorpe Avenue. A small, homely place, Baldock actually enjoyed the food and kept Lisa entertained with tales from his undergraduate years.

For all that he was as relaxed as he had felt in a long time, Baldock still could not resist pointing out that *Apple Crumbel* was spelled wrong on the printed menus.

"The missus," said the proprietor. "She spelled quiche wrong, too." He pointed out the line on the menu which read '*Keesh*'. "I told her, I said, folk on Midthorpe don't want fancy foreign foods like that, anyway."

"Foreign?" Baldock asked. "What's in it?"

"Bacon and egg."

Afterwards, they climbed into Baldock's car and drove back to his mother's.

"I just want to make sure Dad's all right before we shoot off to my place," Lisa said as he pulled up outside the house.

"And I need some clothing," he reminded her as he cut the engine.

Twenty minutes later, they were back out on the street, having assured Janet and Tim that they would be back for lunch no later than one o'clock on Sunday.

Despite Lisa's protests, Baldock insisted upon taking his car. "How many more wheels will it need by tomorrow morning if I leave it here?" he asked as they walked out of his mother's. "I'll follow you."

After Lisa collected her car from the pub, it meant another drive down into Leeds, following broad dual carriageways, many of which Baldock no longer recognised as the network of roads which had encircled the outer edges of the city centre in his younger days. Crossing the river over Crown Point Bridge, she turned off and up past Leeds Minster, the parish church where his grandmother had been married, towards the renowned Kirkgate Market. But before they reached the top of the road, Lisa turned off, Baldock right behind her, along back streets which still housed small to medium-sized businesses and bars.

Vaguely aware that they were headed back toward the lower end of Briggate, Baldock noticed that many of the taller, three and four storey buildings had been converted to living accommodation.

Before they reached the main thoroughfare, however, Lisa turned into River's Edge Wharf, a narrow, cobbled street, with high-rise buildings either side. Following her, Baldock could see the actual river's edge and a range of similar buildings on the other side of the Aire. As his eyes took in the scene before him, he noticed the danger of some drunken driver ending up in the river was averted by a low wall, higher than a car's wheelbase, and therefore capable of stopping any approaching vehicle, but not high enough to restrict the view. He wondered idly what kind of speed he would need to achieve to smash through the wall. It would make a thrilling scene in a Headingley novel.

At the lower end, almost on the river's edge, Lisa stopped, climbed out of her car, and pressed her key fob to a pair of steel gates on the right. They rumbled open, she drove in, followed closely by Baldock, and once in the claustrophobic, enclosed yard, with its dark, arched undercrofts, a throwback to the days when this building had been a mill or warehouse and unloaded barges from the river, she drove into one of her two reserved spots. Baldock waited until she had left her car before reversing in alongside her.

"You won't lose your wheels here, Raymond," she assured him.

While he was willing to agree with her, he had nevertheless been filled with disappointment on their approach to the area.

He remembered these backstreets from his youth, and if the riverside then had been populated with old, decrepit mills and warehouses, little seemed to have changed. For all their secure access and private parking, they were still old, decrepit foundation buildings and no more appealing than the shambling warehouses of his memory.

It was the kind of development, probably pioneered in London's Docklands area, which had sprung up in all the major cities. Even in Norwich there were riverside apartments, mostly on the opposite side of the Wensum from Norwich City FC's Carrow Road ground.

As with all such developments, matters were different as they entered the building and made their way up to the second floor, and Lisa's apartment.

Following her in and along the narrow entrance hall, it opened out into the lounge, and a false Juliet balcony, which afforded a fine view across the river and towards Leeds Bridge. Beyond that iconic landmark and the buildings the other side of the river, the sun blazed in the clear, summer sky, as it moved westward, its reflection sparkling off the still waters of the Aire beneath them.

"I'll just put the kettle on." Lisa disappeared into the small kitchen, leaving Baldock to marvel at this view of his hometown.

In his day, the River Aire had always been a dirty, muddy brown expanse of water trudging its way east to the Humber Estuary. He had crossed it many times, both by car and bus, and even in the cab of his father's lorry when he was a boy, and it never had any appeal. Now, with the development of these modern apartments crowding the old wharfs, there was something peaceful and almost magical about it. In many ways, it reminded him of his home in Norfolk, close to the banks of the Bure. True, the Bure was flanked by grassland and the Norfolk Broads Yacht Club, not the remnants of the Yorkshire wool trade, but the effect upon him was similar. When he returned to Wroxham, it was a haven of serenity, a refuge from the hectic hell of London. Here in Leeds, River's Edge Wharf was the same kind of retreat; a sanctuary from the nightmare of the last twenty-four hours.

And it was augmented by Lisa's taste in modern, yet comfortable furnishings.

"This place must have cost a fortune," he said as she returned from the kitchen. He was immediately embarrassed by his words and hastened to make amends. "I'm sorry, Lisa. I wasn't poking my nose in. Just thinking out loud."

She chuckled. "No problem, Raymond. And as for the cost, I think it was a hundred and sixty-thousand. Like most people, I find the mortgage is a millstone round my neck. I suppose that's not a problem you have."

He could see in her face that the moment she said it, she regretted it and now it was her turn to apologise.

"Sorry, Raymond. That sounds awfully catty. I promise you, I am not envious of your wealth."

"I have a mortgage," he confessed with a generous shrug. "My house cost over four hundred thousand pounds, and my accountant recommended mortgaging it purely for tax purposes. But you're right. It's not a problem to me." He made himself comfortable on a large, pale cream, leather settee. "And just to clear up one or two things, Lisa, I'm not embarrassed by my wealth and I don't apologise for it, but by the same token, I do appreciate I am very lucky."

"Lucky? I think you're an excellent writer. If I said your tales were a bit too gory for me, it was purely a personal thing. I still believe they're well-written."

Genuine applause or another effort to smooth things between them? Baldock decided it did not matter, and affected an air of nonchalance. "Perhaps. Perhaps not. I was lucky, Lisa. I was in the right place at the right time with the right product." In order to draw them to less contentious topics, he asked, "So, what do you do for entertainment here? Walk up into the city?"

"Mostly," she agreed. "But I get a taxi back. Leeds is no more dangerous than, say, London, Birmingham, or Manchester, but it pays not to take chances." The kettle snapped off and she got to her feet. "I'll get that tea."

As the afternoon wore on into the evening, they showered and changed, and then ambled up into the city centre, savouring the warm evening air and the general mood of good cheer the recent weather had brought upon people.

Baldock, as relaxed as he had felt in many months, treated them to dinner at a busy, upmarket restaurant/cocktail bar on Boar Lane, opposite the Trinity Shopping Centre, and throughout a meal of veal escalope, the conversation drifted around many areas, including their present escapades and efforts to track down the source of the Fiagara. After the meal and a couple of drinks in the bar, in deference to her advice on walking the city streets at night, they took a taxi for the short journey back to her apartment.

Over coffee and a conversation steered through safe waters, Baldock found the long hours of the last two days catching up on him, and with the clock reading ten thirty, declared it was time for bed.

"Not," he said good-humouredly, "that I'm hinting at anything."

It was nothing more than the truth. He might have set his

cap at Lisa twenty years ago, but she had matured into one of those fine-looking women, bent on her independence, and any suggestion of a sexual nature would, he was certain, be immediately rebuffed.

She led him to the hall, and turned into the first room on the right. "This is where you sleep," she said, gesturing at a king-sized divan.

Baldock was surprised. On a dressing table beneath the windows stood a range of perfumes and other accoutrements, all unmistakably female, and the room had about it, an air of being lived in. "But… but surely, this must be your room."

He turned to face her, and she pushed him back onto bed.

"Lisa—"

He had no time to say more as she leapt upon him, straddling his waist, collapsing forward and locking her lips to his.

Soon, breaking the kiss, she knelt upright, still pinning him to the mattress. Her skirt had ridden up revealing arousing black mesh at the top of her hold-ups, and above that, the bare, tanned skinned of her upper thigh. Baldock was uncertain of the colour of her knickers, because he felt that a gentleman would not look that far up.

She stripped off her blouse.

"Lisa—"

"Shut up, Raymond," she ordered, and threw the garment to one side. She quickly snapped off her bra, baring her small but impressive breasts, standing proud without support, the nipples erect. Then she pressed herself back down on him and began to fiddle around his rapidly growing member. Pulling her panties to one side, preparing to guide him home, she breathed, "I've waited twenty years for this, and you don't get out of here until you get out of me."

Chapter Ten

The waters of the Aire were just as still the following day when Baldock sat before the open Juliet balcony savouring the morning sun.

A narrow boat appeared beneath the Centenary Bridge, a footway over the river a hundred and fifty yards from him. As the boat plodded along, stirring the waters in its shallow wake, Baldock's lively imagination carried him to Amsterdam and its network of canals.

The sound of Lisa moving around somewhere behind him, automatically conjured other images, more in keeping with Amsterdam's salacious and often-unjust reputation.

As memories of the night assailed him, Baldock was a satisfied individual. Sex with Lisa was all he had imagined it would be and more besides. And assuming the woman was not faking, her moans and cries and urgent demands for more led him to believe she had found it mutually gratifying.

She came into the living room, draped her arms around his shoulder and nuzzled his neck. Baldock felt his hormones stirring again at the musky scent of a night's sleep emanating from her.

"It was worth the wait," she husked.

"For me too," he assured her.

Lisa giggled. "But don't think you're going back to Norfolk without a repeat performance."

"I, er, I wouldn't dream of it." He felt a mixture of excitement at the prospect and embarrassment at her openness. In his circles there were some things one simply did not talk about and the previous night's exercise was one such taboo. Gently moving her arms away, he asked, "Shall I make coffee?"

"If you don't mind. Cappuccino for me. I'll just take a shower."

In fact, Baldock was glad of the opportunity to be doing something else. It helped take his mind from the tumult of carnal thoughts and near-pornographic images bouncing round his head.

Disparaging rumours appeared in the press now and then, and he refused to rise to them, but in truth, he was no stranger to sex, merely to relationships. He had never had what could be described as a regular or steady girlfriend. Most of his encounters were simply that: one-night stands. Before his rise to fame, there had been one woman who hung around for a couple of months before she, too, found him boring out of bed, and wandered off in search of more stimulating company. Since he became well-known there had been a number of different women, but by then it was he who refused to become involved.

"Wary of fortune hunters," he had told his agent when she asked.

Would Lisa come under that heading? Or was he simply being presumptuous, imagining that one night of carnal bliss, evidently as satisfactory for her as it had been for him, would lead to a long-term and lasting relationship?

He poured out two cappuccinos, and moved back to the table by the windows from where he could overlook the river once more.

There was, he realised, a large stumbling block to any potential relationship. Midthorpe. Lisa loved the area, but forty-eight hours on from his return, nothing had happened to persuade him he needed a permanent return.

He was still musing on such matters and wondering how he could broach them with Lisa, when she returned, dressed in a tight top and a knee length skirt. With so much of her legs on display, he felt his libido limbering up yet again, and in order to maintain control, asked, "With regard to the, er, Fiagara question, is there any more we can do?"

"Lots." Sipping on her cappuccino, she nodded. "Well, some. I think we should try Shippy again."

"He's in hospital," Baldock pointed out. It came out more bluntly than he intended, thanks largely to the tang of her perfume exciting his olfactory nerve and his insistent sexual longing.

"Was in hospital," Lisa corrected. "Dad was discharged yesterday afternoon. Shippy is younger and, we can assume, fitter, so he probably wasn't far behind Dad. He'll be home, Raymond."

"I think that kind of thing is best left to the police."

Now she shook her head, her ponytail jiggling delightfully from side to side, just like it had...

Lisa's words cut off his heated thoughts.

"You're really out of touch, aren't you? The first thing Shippy will do is refuse to speak without a solicitor. It's Sunday and Kramer will have hell's teeth of a job finding a lawyer. But we can make him speak to us." She grinned maliciously. "I'll twist his arm."

The doubt must have registered on his face, and she immediately went on to lecture him.

"Raymond, four men have been floored by this stuff. And we don't know how serious John Taplin and Malcolm Norris are. Someone has to find the source and stop it, and when it comes to Midthorpe, the police are more likely to mark it 'run like hell' than 'urgent'. I work there, remember. My dad and your mum live there." She hesitated a moment. "Or are you secretly scared of the estate and the people?"

"Scared?" He grunted out a little laugh. "I may hate the place, but I don't fear it. I never did. Even when things were at their worst."

"I should have guessed when you tried to outface Gary Lipton, shouldn't I?"

Lisa leaned back to check an ornate wall clock. The action thrust out her breasts and Baldock shivered. He really would have to get a hold of himself... but even the phrasing of the thought sent his desire into orbit.

"It's half past nine," she told him and drank up her coffee. "Shall we make a move?"

"A bit early for Midthorpers, isn't it?" beyond these few

words, the thought echoed round his head. *What I really want is your body again.*

"Not when Shippy and his missus have a houseful of kids. Besides, we need to catch him before he makes for a Sunday lunchtime session in The Midden."

Baldock, too, drank his coffee. "Shall we take my car?"

"If you're happy that the wheels will be safe."

He smiled and collected the cups. "I have Grunny out looking for them, and thanks to you, Gary Lipton safeguarding the replacements."

***

Shipston appeared at the door unkempt and unshaven. Overweight, looking haggard and bleary-eyed, as if they had just got him out of bed, his voice was as faint and hoarse as Tim's had been, but he steadfastly refused to speak to them.

"Not here," he insisted. Meet me at the boating lake in the park in half an hour. If it's safe, I'll talk to you."

"Shippy—" Baldock began, only to be cut off.

"All these years haven't done your hearing much good, Ballcock. Boating lake. Park. Half an hour." And with that, he shut the door on them.

Midthorpe Park sat to the north of the estate, an oasis of green in the general clutter of residential properties. With a municipal golf course attached, its well-tended grassed areas centred on what had been a boating lake many years previous, but which now resembled an overgrown and over-large duck pond. Were it not for the concrete paths encircling the pond, and the lack of boating activity, the infestation of reed would have persuaded Baldock that he was looking at one of his beloved Norfolk Broads.

To one side was a small, children's playground, which had been there in one guise or another, since long before his mother was born.

"Wasn't there some kind of wooden shelter there, too?" Baldock asked as they climbed out of his car near the park's café.

"Knocked down before it fell down," Lisa assured him.

The council still maintained a presence in the park, tending the tennis courts and bowling greens, aerating the waters of the pond, and maintaining fresh and colourful flowerbeds. Beyond their pound where machinery and materials were stored, there were paths, some tarmac, others no more than routes which had been worn down by constant use, led off into Midthorpe Woods, a large spread of woodland which had always served as a natural adventure playground for Midthorpe children.

Midthorpe Colliery, which had been located at the far end of the woods from the park, was history.

"So is the quarry," Lisa said, reminding Baldock of the large pond and sheer sides of limestone and granite which had been another favourite haunt of the local children. "We used to go skinny dipping there when we were teenagers."

"I don't think I did."

She laughed. "No surprise there, then."

She linked his arm as they walked into the café, where she secured a table for them outside, while he went in for soft drinks.

Joining her a minute later, he felt relaxed. The sun shone from a clear sky, the temperature was rising and there were few people in evidence. For the first time in a long time, he was under no pressure.

"Then there was Virgin's Valley," Lisa said. She gave another throaty laugh. "Many a girl took her trolleys off for the first time there."

Baldock struggled once more to bury his craving for her. "Somewhere in the woods, isn't it?"

"Well, it was. Probably overgrown now. I'm not sure. It was only a small clearing, but everyone used to go there for a bit of the other."

"I don't think I did," he repeated, causing her to laugh yet again.

She reached across the table and took his hand, playing with his fingers. "Oh, Raymond, you could have taken me there any time you wanted. All you had to do was say."

"I'm beginning to regret what I missed."

Her response was coy, yet inviting, at once modest and laden with promise. "Perhaps it's time to catch up."

Baldock was not sure how to answer, but he was saved a potentially embarrassing situation by the rattle of Shippy's minibus trundling towards them.

He parked adjacent to Baldock's Mercedes, climbed out and looked around.

"Have to make sure I weren't followed, didn't I?" he said as he invited them to walk with him. His voice still sounded like a poor imitation of Marlon Brando in *The Godfather*.

Carrying their soft drinks, they tagged along as he began to circle the pond.

"I wish you'd stop behaving like some supergrass," Baldock complained. "You do know you've poisoned four men... including yourself."

"Yeah, well, it's not my fault, is it? I mean I only buy them."

"Who from?" Lisa demanded.

"That's for me to know and keep my trap shut."

"My father was one of those you poisoned," Lisa snapped. "Someone will pay for it."

Shippy rounded on her and Baldock prepared to intervene if he had to.

"Then I'll pay for it. What do you want? Your fiver back?" Shippy dug into his pocket.

"Stick the fiver. When I said someone has to pay for it, I meant answer for it, and right now the trail ends with you."

"Then let it end there. You try taking it further and I'll..."

Shippy trailed off, looking up at Baldock and down at Lisa. It was if it had just occurred to him that Baldock was bigger and fitter and Lisa was tougher.

"I can't tell you anything. You don't know these people. To me it's pocket money. To them, it's a business and I don't want to disappear like Nate Perry."

Now he sounded even more like *Don Corleone*.

While Baldock mused on the delivery, Lisa was more interested in the implication behind Shippy's words.

"What does Nathan Perry have to do with this?"

"I...er... I don't know. But I don't think he left home. Not of his own accord, anyway."

Lisa was about to tackle him again, but Baldock intervened.

"Let's not get side-tracked. Shippy, if you don't talk to us, you'll have to talk to the police, and if you don't talk to them, you could end up in prison for attempted murder."

"Then I'll end up inside. Better that than pushing up the weeds, innit?" His stance softened a little. "Listen, Lisa, I'm sorry about your dad. If I'd known, I wouldn't have sold the pill to Janet. But I can't say more than that."

"So you make these pills do you?" Lisa demanded.

"Er... yes. I do."

"And Kirsty knows about it?"

"Er... yes, she does."

"Then how come she told us you buy them?"

"I... er... she got it wrong. I make 'em."

"But you just told us you buy them." Baldock felt his patience wearing thin. "For heaven's sake, Shippy, what are you afraid of?"

"Them," Shippy answered truthfully and quickly. "You got away from this sodding estate, Ballcock, so you don't know how bad it's got. These bastards won't just stop at beating you up, you know."

Baldock fixed Shippy's gaze with his own. "Tell me who they are and I'll show you how to stand up to them."

"Forget it. Just send the cops. Let 'em wall me up."

Shippy turned on his heels and marched off towards his minibus.

They were at the far end of the boating lake from where they watched him climb into his bus, fire the engine and drive off, his exhaust pouring out a cloud of dark smoke as it chugged up the rise to the park gates.

"He was terrified," Lisa said.

Baldock noted that her tones were puzzled. "You find that surprising?"

"Shippy isn't the hardest nut on the tree, but he's not soft.

I don't know what, or who he's mixed up with, Raymond, but it sounds serious."

"Then we should do like he suggests and pass it on to Inspector Kramer."

"I think you're right."

They, too, ambled back towards the café, but when they reached the end of the boating lake, Lisa stopped.

"It's too early to go back to your mother's," she declared, "and there are things we need to talk about."

"Concerning, er, us?"

Lisa giggled and repeated, "It's too early to go back to your mother's and it's too early to talk about us."

They continued making their way back to the car park.

"Shippy," Lisa said, her voice breaking into the silence so suddenly that Baldock was startled. "He hinted that Nate Perry's disappearance was to do with the distribution of these fake pills."

"He also backtracked quite quickly when you pressed him."

"Everything he said was a waste of his breath and our time." Lisa stopped, turned and looked up into Baldock's eyes. "Nathan went missing at the beginning of the year, Raymond. Suppose he didn't just take off. Suppose he was murdered like Shippy suggested."

He held her by the shoulders, and tried to smile encouragingly. "I'll repeat what I've said many times before. I write detective stories, Lisa. I don't solve crimes. It's no concern of ours."

"Wrong. It is a concern of mine. I live here, I work here, I feel for the people of Midthorpe, and the last thing we want is organised crime or the gangs getting a bigger grip on the area than they have already."

"Then we pass it on to the police."

They arrived back at Baldock's car only to find the alarm tweeting for attention, and the real nearside wheel missing, the axle propped up on bricks.

Killing the alarm, Baldock took out his mobile phone. "Oh, for God's sake. This is getting beyond a joke."

"They do seem to be targeting you," Lisa commented.

A rotund, middle aged man, spectacles perched on his nose, the peak of his flat cap hiding his eyes, his right hand clasping a lead on the end of which was a Jack Russell terrier, stepped down from the cafeteria's exterior tables and grumbled at Baldock. "It's been like that for the last twenty minutes. It's driving Joe up the wall." He nodded down at the dog, which sat patiently and silently waiting for the prompt to move on.

"I'm sorry," Baldock apologised. "The next time someone chooses to take my wheels, I'll get them to let me know in advance so I disable the alarm. Did you see who took the wheel?"

"Oh, I saw 'em all right. They said they were taking it away to put a new tyre on. One of 'em was coloured."

Lisa frowned. "And what colour was he? Green? Purple?"

"You know what I mean."

"Asian or Afro-Caribbean?" Baldock asked.

"By the sound of his accent, Yorkshire." The man looked down at his dog. "Come on, Joe. Let's get a move on."

Watching him and his dog walk off, Baldock got through to the tyre company and ordered a replacement wheel and tyre.

"You again? Have you thought about having the wheels welded to the axles?"

"I'll take it into consideration. In the meantime, what can you do about it?"

"Well first off, I'll take your credit card number – again – then I'll send a lad out – again – and then I'll ring the travel agent, and upgrade to first class."

Baldock cut the call and reported to Lisa. "It'll be an hour or so before they get here and get the job done."

She took his hand. "Shall we take a walk, then?"

The path ahead, dirt and cinder in place of tarmac, forked. Lisa drifted off to the right and Baldock followed. The woods began to close round them, larch, beech, elm climbing up, spreading as far as the overcrowding would allow, and underfoot, either side of the narrow path, soft mats of grass fought for ground with the fern and bush of the forest floor. The air was heady with many scents, and from somewhere nearby came the cooing of a wood pigeon.

"The night Nathan disappeared," Baldock asked. "Who were the friends he was going to meet?"

"Peter Lipton and Josh Allen."

He snorted. "And no one took his disappearance seriously. If I were a betting man—"

"You'd put your money on a pair of evens favourites," Lisa interrupted. "And you'd be wrong."

Lisa stumbled over a clod of grass. Baldock reached out an arm and stopped her falling. As she came upright, she turned into him, and they kissed.

"I've met them," he reminded her.

"But you don't know them. They're ordinary teenagers, Raymond. Not hardened criminals." Her eyes strayed to the right and a small glade in the woods. A smile broke on her lips and all thoughts of Nathan Perry, Peter Lipton and Josh Allen were forgotten. "Oh look. Virgin's Valley." She turned back to Baldock and pulled herself close, reaching her arms up and around his neck. "This is where I wanted you, Raymond. All those years ago. This is where I wanted you to bring me and take me."

"Well, yes, but—"

"Come on. Let's do it now."

His natural reticence enveloped him. "Lisa, this is a public park. It's the middle of summer. There'll be people—"

"Just as there always were, but it didn't stop anyone. Besides, it really is a valley. You can't be seen from here." She took his hand and practically dragged him along.

Ten yards off from the path, the ground dipped. Lisa hurried down, pulling Baldock behind her. And as they made the middle of the glade, where the grasses had been flattened by years of human sexual interaction, she turned into him. "I want it now, Raymond. Your best ever effort."

She took a pace back, ready to drag them both to the mossy ground, but as she did so, she tripped over a protruding tree root and fell backwards.

Baldock reached out a hand to help her up, and then froze. "Oh God. I think I'm going to be sick."

Lisa smiled at the notion. "If that's what the promise of sex in the woods does to you, Raymond, maybe we should…"

She trailed off and followed his horrified eyes. He was looking to his left, her right, staring at the ground. The colour really had drained from his cheeks, and he looked a little green around the gills.

Lisa turned her head slowly to her right. Her eyes opened wide. A chill rushed through her, and she, too, felt like she was about to vomit.

It was not a tree root she had tripped over. Instead, jutting up from the undergrowth, with only remnants of skin, hanging like torn, ragged cloth from it, was a human hand.

Chapter Eleven

Inspector Kramer settled onto a chair at Janet's kitchen table, placed her briefcase at her elbow and took out her notebook.

She had greeted them pleasantly, asking after Tim's health, and reassuring Janet that no charges would be brought against her. She then asked to speak to Baldock and Lisa alone.

"I don't want to disturb you anymore than I have to, Mr Baldock, Ms Yeoman," she said when Janet and Tim had left the kitchen for the front room, "and I know you gave a brief statement to the attending officers in the woods, but things have moved on, so I need a more detailed account. How are you both feeling?"

"Fairly well," Baldock confessed, "but I'm afraid Mother's excellent cooking went to waste. Neither I nor Lisa have eaten anything since…" He trailed off with a shudder.

Over four hours had passed since the terrible discovery.

When Lisa realised what Baldock was staring at, she practically threw him off, and rushed away, as if she expected the hand to follow her. She was all set to leave the woods altogether, run for it, when Baldock stopped her.

"We have to call the police, Lisa."

"I know, but can we not do it from the car?"

"And if someone else happens on this… this…" He could not bring himself to say it. "I told you, I've worked with the police in Norfolk. They will want this area preserving as far as is possible. If we leave and someone else lets Midthorpe know about it, the place will be crawling with ghouls and souvenir hunters by the time the pubs have opened. We have to call them."

"I can't stay here staring at that hand."

"No. Me neither. Come on. Let's get out of the clearing and wait on the path." As they hurried away from the ghastly scene, Baldock handed her his keys. "You go back to the car and wait there. I'll stay here."

Lisa shook her head. "No, no. I'll wait with you."

The uniformed officers arrived ten minutes after he called them, soon followed by the forensic team. A sympathetic woman constable took their statement and contact details while the scientific support people erected white tents around the macabre scene.

"Would you please tell Detective Inspector Kramer that we need to speak to her," Baldock insisted.

"I think Ms Kramer might be a bit too busy, sir," the constable replied.

"She knows who we are, and we have information linked to an incident she's investigating which we were, er, sort of, involved in."

The woman constable tapped her notebook with her pen. "Oh, yes? Maybe I should reconsider letting you go home."

"Constable, please," Lisa put in, "we came across this poor man... woman... whoever, purely by accident, but we do have information for her. If you ask her to find us at Raymond's mother's home."

"The address I just gave you," Baldock said.

"All right." The constable was obviously still not happy. "You can go for now, but don't wander from the Midthorpe area."

From there, Baldock and Lisa had returned to his car, now with all four wheels in place, and drove back to his mother's where they waited for news, but as he indicated to Inspector Kramer, neither of them had any appetite as a consequence of which, they had foregone lunch.

The detective oozed sympathy. "It can affect you like that." In a more business-like manner, she went on, "Can I ask, what were you doing in the glade to disturb the body?"

Baldock blushed and looked away.

Lisa groaned. "If I told you that clearing is known as Virgin's Valley, would we need to draw you a diagram?"

Now Kramer blushed. "Oh. I see. Well, you should be careful in those woods. We've had reports of peeping toms there."

Lisa felt obliged to explain. "We weren't actually, er, at it, so any voyeur watching us won't have got his fix, will he?"

"Quite."

In an effort to bring some focus to the discussion, Baldock asked, "Have you identified the body?"

Busy making notes, Kramer did not immediately answer. But she did pause for a second, taking them both in with a non-committal stare before going back to her notes. Eventually, she put her pen away, and faced them.

"We think we've identified him. There are no facial features left to go on, so we won't be sure until we have dental records or a DNA profile." Kramer crossed her hands in her lap. "How well do you know the people of Midthorpe, Ms Yeoman?"

"I don't live here these days," Lisa admitted. "I have a place by the river in the city. But I am the resident counsellor at the Health Centre, so I get to know most of the tittle-tattle."

Kramer nodded and turned to Baldock. "And you, sir?"

"I'm currently resident in Norfolk. I haven't lived on Midthorpe for almost twenty years." He purposely buried the sense of pride he normally felt when he said those words. "I know the older people, of course, but I wouldn't say I'm particularly familiar with the younger end."

"Right. So you won't know anything about Nathan Perry?"

Lisa's face drained white. Baldock merely shrugged, but his agile mind was already ticking over, recalling their conversation with Shippy.

"I knew he disappeared some months ago." He took in Kramer's suspicious look. "I caught it on the news early in the year."

"That's right," the detective agreed. "We had reports at the beginning of the year. Most people assumed he had just run off. That's not unusual for a sixteen-year-old, especially when they live on Midthorpe, but if he had, he was living under the radar. No sightings, no messages from him to his family, no claim for benefits anywhere. However, if we're right about this morning's find, then he hadn't run off. He was murdered."

Lisa turned even paler and looked as if she was about to reel.

Notwithstanding the shocking discovery, Baldock felt completely detached from the new revelations. "If you're right? You mean you're not certain?"

"All we have, Mr Baldock, are some fragments of clothing and what's left of a pair of Adidas trainers. One of our liaison officers is with the Perrys right now. The shoe size is right, the material of the jeans... well, we'll have to wait for tests. And, of course, it will take several days for conclusive DNA tests."

"And it was definitely murder?"

"Nothing is definite, sir. We'll have to wait for the pathologist's report. All we can say at the moment is there is no apparent skull trauma. The forensic bods have found pellets from a 12-gauge shotgun around the body, but it's too early to say whether they were fired at him or into the ground when he was buried there."

Lisa seized on a faint ray of hope. "If so, could it be a suicide?"

Kramer shrugged. "Highly unlikely. Suicides usually place the barrel in their mouth or under the chin, and the damage to the skull would be visible. In any case, suicides ten not to bury themselves in Midthorpe Woods. I'm guessing murder." Kramer took both of them in with concerned eyes. "I'd be grateful if you didn't say anything to anyone about this just now. You know how quickly speculation can turn to wild rumours these day, and if the media get hold it, we'll have every vigilante group in South Leeds looking for a nutter with a shotgun."

"I assume there will be plenty of such nutters on Midthorpe," Baldock commented, much to Lisa's displeasure.

"Now, sir, according to the uniformed officer who took your statement, you wanted to see me. You had information for me."

"Yes, and I think it may be even more important now." Lisa dug into her bag, and came out with the Fiagara pill she had bought from Kirsty Shipston, and handed it over.

"Fiagara," Baldock announced.

Slipping on a pair of forensic gloves, Kramer unwrapped it and turned it over once or twice in her hands. "Where did you get this?"

"Shippy," Lisa replied. "Michael Shipston. Well, we got it from his wife. He was still in hospital at the time. He sold the pill to Raymond's mother on Friday night. Have you spoken to him, yet?"

"We tried." The detective scowled. "He was too fast for us. We tracked him down to the infirmary, but when we got there, he had a lawyer who insisted he couldn't speak to us until Monday at the earliest. When his throat is better."

"He had no problem speaking to us," Baldock reported. "Well, no *physical* problem."

Lisa backed him up. "He also intimated that he may know something about Nathan Perry's disappearance."

Kramer's features turned to a look of thunder on this double revelation. "What? You've spoken..." She took a deep breath and let it out in an irritated hiss. "Tell me exactly what happened."

Between them, they reconstructed the conversation as best they could remember. Kramer did not interrupt, but made occasional notes, and when they had finished, she got on the phone to her colleagues and ordered Shippy's arrest.

Baldock, his writer's brain working full stretch, watched and listened with interest, and as Kramer shut off the phone, he asked, "What precisely would Shippy be arrested for, Inspector? Supplying drugs?"

"That's a difficult question to answer, Mr Baldock, because right now, I don't know, but I can tell you that, unless this Fiagara turns up something, Shipston is unlikely to be guilty of supplying drugs." Flipping open the lid of her briefcase she came out with a sealed evidence bag containing several blue pills wrapped in bubblepack. "We found these in amongst what was left of the clothing on the body you unearthed. We won't know what they are until we've had them analysed, but according to medical reports on all four men, your father, Ms Yeoman, Shipston included, they've swallowed nothing more than drain cleaner, which probably got there by mistake and which is toxic, not narcotic. The packaging is amateurish, so we don't think they're from a genuine laboratory: not even a criminal one. They could be narcotics, or worse, and the colour suggests Viagra, or possibly more of this substitute, Fiagara. But it doesn't have the letter F on it. Would either of you know the difference?"

For the life of him, Baldock could not imagine pills worse than hard drugs. He took his irritation out on Kramer's question. "At my age, I don't need artificial stimulants, genuine or fake."

"My dad would know," Lisa said. "I'll go get him."

While she left, Baldock and the inspector sat in silence, until she broke it.

"You've found real life bodies a little different to describing it in your novels, Mr Baldock."

"Much worse, but from a writer's point of view, no matter how ghastly an experience, it can always be put to use. You'll be a good few days waiting for the scientific reports, I imagine."

"It could be weeks. Even months. We're assuming it's young Perry. If it isn't, it could take forever to ID the poor sod."

"So what do you do in the meantime?"

"Work on the assumption that it is Nathan Perry and try to put together his last movements. It won't be easy. The initial reports suggest that he went out to meet his friends, but they say he never showed up."

Lisa returned with Tim and Janet.

Kramer handed Tim the pills. "Mr Yeoman, can you identify these pills as a batch of the Fiagara you took?"

Tim studied them and shook his head. His voice still not

much better than a hoarse whisper, he said, "Fiagara is the same size and colour, but it has a letter F stamped on it. Like that one." He pointed to the sample pill his daughter had given the policewoman. "These have nowt. I don't know what they are, but I've never seen Fiagara like that."

Kramer took them back and dropped the bag in her case along with the Fiagara. "Thank you. I guess we'll just have to wait for the analysis." Packing up her notebook and dropping it into the case, she stood up. "Well, thank you all. I'm sorry you had such a shock, Ms Yeoman, and you Mr Baldock, but I'm sure you'll soon get over it, and I do appreciate your help."

Baldock showed her to the door. When he returned, he found Lisa discussing events in Midthorpe Woods with her father, and his mother anxiously washing up pots, her brow knotted in furious concentration, her lips moving soundlessly in the delicate equivalent of chewing spit.

"Mother?"

"I'll have to go see Carol. The poor woman... that poor boy."

"I'll take you," Baldock said. "Lisa, would you and your dad be all right here while I take mother—"

"We'll come with you," Tim interrupted.

"No, Tim," Janet insisted. "You have to take it easy."

"Don't talk so soft. I'm as right as I'm ever gonna be. No worse than a sore throat now. And I've known Carol as long as you have. We'll come with you."

Baldock recognised a Midthorpe standoff when he saw one. His mother determined that Tim should be resting to recuperate, Tim determined that he was as tough as they come. At length, Janet backed down with a brisk nod, and dried her hands on a tea towel.

"If you feel unwell, I'll have Raymond bring you home."

Janet made a brief phone call to Carol Perry, and they climbed into Baldock's Mercedes for the short journey to the Perrys' house on Nimmons Terrace, where they found a clutch of cars parked outside, amongst which was a police patrol car.

The house was full of people, many of whom Baldock did not know. Carol Perry was the same age as his mother, but with her grey hair pulled into a tight bun, and gnarled hands twisting and knotting a handkerchief, she looked much older. She sat with her son and daughter-in-law. Baldock did not know Angela Perry, but he had been at school around the same time as Vince, her husband and Nathan's father. He sat on the settee staring dumbly into space and barely registered Baldock's trite words of condolence.

While his mother and Tim sat down to sympathise with Carol, and Lisa spoke to the police officers, Baldock exchanged a brief word with Elaine, Carol's youngest daughter, and one of those women who had made his life hell at school, then took himself into the back garden.

The air of grief and depression which hung over the room was another new experience for him. His coloured, mental model of Midthorpe was of homes where men and women cocked a snook at authority while watching Sky TV on stolen boxes, or plotted their next crime/benefit fraud. The idea that they suffered the same emotions, good and bad, as people everywhere, was almost alien, and again demonstrated, if only to himself, his inbuilt prejudice against the estate and its population.

The garden provided him with another surprise. He was used to seeing his mother's back garden well kept, but nothing particularly special. Vince and Angela Perry had done a lot of work here. It was not a large area, but there were paved paths wandering past small flowerbeds, leading to a broad patio area at the bottom of the garden, where table and chairs sheltered under a small, canvas gazebo.

He was also surprised to find Terry Hardwick at the table, a couple of large carrier bags on the paving stones next to him.

"Baldock." Hardwick nodded a greeting.

"Hardwick." Baldock took the chair opposite. And glanced down at the bags.

"Baking supplies," Hardwick said. "Flour, dried fruits, colouring, sugar, icing. You know the kind of thing."

"Ah. Of course. Your wife likes to bake cakes, does she?"

"Not so's you'd notice. To be honest, they're mostly mine. I love baking. Make my own bread most of the time."

Baldock nodded disinterestedly. "Are you the, er, official school representative, here to sympathise with Nathan's parents?"

"Hell, no. I'm the boy's uncle. I married Elaine Perry. Remember? I told you on Friday."

"Oh yes. Of course. My apologies."

"I just said a quick hello, offered my sympathies and came out here to get out of the way."

At a loss for something to say, Baldock went on, "According to the police, they're not absolutely certain it's Nathan."

"Are they not? Dunno. I haven't spoken to them. But it's him," Hardwick's features were set grim and dark. "Recognised those tatty trainers right away. He wore nowt but them at school. And I reckon the bits of material they found were his jeans. Skinny jeans from Next. Nate always wore skinny jeans and always bought them from Next."

"You knew him well?"

"Better than I know his parents. He was in one or two of my classes."

Once again, Baldock's mind slipped automatically into research mode and in an effort to satisfy it, his next question was designed to glean information. "Isn't that a little odd? I mean were you never worried about accusations of nepotism?"

He had no qualms about using words such as 'nepotism'. He blandly assumed that most people on Midthorpe would not understand it, but Hardwick had a degree, and as a teacher, he could be expected to enjoy a much larger vocabulary.

"Not really. There's no problem teaching the lad. Hell, for all anyone knew, I could have been tutoring him privately anyway. Assessments can be quirky, but I handed him over to a colleague for them. The Head was aware of our relationship, and she supervised the assessment process. It's completely above board. The Head's son and two daughters all attend Midthorpe and no one accuses her." Hardwick laughed without humour. "Behavioural problems can be a bit embarrassing, though. They tend to reflect on family, even extended family such as me."

"I can imagine." Baldock slotted the information into the back of his mind. There was no telling when it might come in handy, especially if Detective Inspector Headingley were called to a murder in a school. "Nate was badly behaved?"

"Not in school especially, but teenage lads are... well, you know."

Baldock knew. He often wondered why he had been so well-behaved as a teenager, but he knew the answer. His mother had pointed it out to him two days previously. When everyone else was playing the tearaway, he preferred to immerse himself in the absurd picture of Great Britain as a world power as painted by Ian Fleming. It pleased him to think that the country still ruled a quarter of the world. It also, he reflected, kept him off the streets and as such, out of trouble.

Bringing his thoughts back into focus, he said, "You're aware that police have found what appear to be drugs close to the body? It looks as if Nate was selling them."

"Hmm, yes." Hardwick's features darkened further. "I'm not surprised."

"Really?"

Hardwick took out a cigarette and made a great fuss of lighting it, and then offered the pack to Baldock, who refused.

"I don't smoke."

"Sensible man."

"You said you were not surprised. About the drugs, I mean."

Hardwick took in a large lungful of smoke and let it out with a hiss, watching the light, summer breeze take it away from under the gazebo. He looked around, as if checking that there was no one within earshot, and then leaned forward and lowered his voice.

"I said he wasn't badly behaved in school, but out of it... well... He was in with a bad crowd. Lipton and Allen. They were the ones giving you S-H-one-T on Friday afternoon." Hardwick sat back. "I don't know how well you know the people on this estate, but those two are of the worst kind."

"I know both their fathers." Baldock's features darkened too. "I've known Lipton's father for years. Too many years."

"Then you'll understand what I mean." Hardwick sat back. "If anyone could get hold of a shotgun, it would be them. And if any pair were candidates for drug dealing, it would be them. And if anyone could lead Nate into trouble, it would be them. Especially, Peter."

"Maybe, maybe not," Baldock said. "Right now, the police are picking up Michael Shipston. Er, you know Shippy?"

Hardwick shook his head. "Never heard of hm. Local is he?"

"A true, renegade Midthorper."

"Hmm. Well, let's hope it gets the cops somewhere, eh? Must have been a bit of shock for you, finding the body like that."

"Not one I'd care to repeat," Baldock replied. "I think I'm speaking for Lisa, too, when I say that."

As if he had summoned her, Lisa appeared and delivered a sympathetic smile on Hardwick. "Hello, Terry, and my condolences on your loss."

"No great loss to me, Lisa. I'm a distant relative, and only then by marriage." Hardwick drew on his cigarette. "I was just explaining to Raymond how Nate got himself mixed up with a bad crowd."

She frowned. "Call me soft or stupid, but I don't like to hear boys like Pete Lipton and Josh Allen labelled as 'bad'."

"All right," Hardwick agreed. "Let's say headstrong."

Now she smiled sweetly before speaking directly to Baldock. "Your mother and my dad are ready if you are, Raymond."

"Yes. Right." He stood up. "Well, nice talking to you, Hardwick."

"And you. And if you ever feel like dropping by the school

again to waste your breath, please let us know."
 "I will."

Chapter Twelve

"Bernie, I appreciate how difficult this is, but what do you expect me to do? It's a clear case of murder, I found the body, and I can hardly walk away from it until the police say so, and that is not going to happen today."

With his mobile pressed to his ear, listening to his agent jabbering at him, Baldock felt he could have come up with a better excuse for not going home. Although Bernie was not aware of it, Kramer had made it clear that she did not suspect him or Lisa of any involvement in either the Fiagara fiasco or the killing of Nathan Perry... should that turn out to be the body in the woods. He could get into his car and go home whenever he chose. He could certainly be in Norwich in time for the planned appearance at a large bookstore tomorrow afternoon if he wished.

But he did not wish. He would rather hang on at least one more day.

He listened to Bernie rant about broken promises and the backlash from Shortly Publishing who had gone to the trouble of delivering extra copies of *Headingley and the Valentine Slasher* to the shop in question.

"You're not thinking this through, Bernie. By tomorrow, this will make not only the local news, but the national channels, too. You're always telling me that there's no such thing as bad publicity. Can you imagine the headlines?"

Baldock certainly could. He had not been a journalist for nothing.

Crime king in real-life murder inquiry. Headingley creator finds body in woods. Baldock and the buried body.

The real reason for his reluctance to leave Leeds stepped into the living room as the telephone debate with Bernie ran round in another circle. Lisa raised her eyebrows at him, asking how he was getting on.

He frowned and gave the slightest shake of his head as he answered Bernie.

"You're my agent. It's what you get paid for," he said when he could get a word in. "And I'm not suggesting we cancel. I'm saying we should defer. If you give this story time to spread nationally, especially if you and Shortly help spread the tale, and then speak to the shop manager, rearrange for, say, next Monday, by which time half the world will know that Inspector Headingley's creator has stumbled upon a real murder, I guarantee we'll add another ten percent in sales. Maybe more. Put it that way to Masters, and even that slimy, money-grabbing cretin will see the logic. He'll have his publicity department on it by lunchtime tomorrow."

Again he paused to listen, while Lisa sat in the armchair by the fire, waiting for him to conclude the call.

"Yes, yes, I know I shouldn't call him names like that, but you know how far he gets up my nose. And quite frankly, I hold both him and you responsible for this mess. You arranged the talk to the children at Midthorpe Comprehensive, and with hindsight, it was bloody stupid to arrange a book signing two hundred miles away so close to the school thing."

There was another pause and Baldock raised his eyes to the ceiling as if begging for divine intervention.

"Of course I've been staying with my mother Do you seriously imagine that I could come all this way and not spend the weekend with her? And it's not her fault that this body turned up in a nearby park."

There were several more rallies in this game of verbal tennis before Baldock finally cut the connection and dropped the smartphone in his shirt pocket.

"Someone's not happy with you?" Lisa asked.

"Put it this way, I'll be lucky to get a birthday card from her."

"You could have gone home, Raymond."

"Yes, I could, but to be honest, Lisa, having uncovered the body, with your, er, help, I need to know more about it. That kid has been dumped in the ground, and it just doesn't seem right. No matter how he died, he was entitled to a Christian burial."

"And the chances of putting a real murder to bed with Inspector Headingley hovering in the background of your mind, is too good to pass up, isn't it?"

"I'd be lying if I didn't agree that this is excellent research material," he admitted before realising that Lisa's words were dripping with cynical disapproval. "You don't think I should?"

"It's not that. It's just that everything seems to be business with you."

He tried to smile pleasantly, but he feared it came out as more of a leer. "Not everything." Quickly changing tack, he asked, "Have you eaten, yet?"

"Your mother just made me some toast. It's helping settle my stomach. You should try to eat too. I know it's—"

Janet burst into the room, interrupting Lisa.

"Raymond. Quickly. Someone's propped a bike up against your car and I think they're fooling around with your wheels again."

Baldock leapt to his feet, but he was slower than Lisa, who was on her way out into the street while he was still making his way to the door.

As he reached the garden gate, he could see Lisa haranguing whoever was trying to steal the wheel. Then she backed off, and the young man stood upright, facing her, the unmistakable, ugly black shape of an automatic pistol in his hand, aimed at her.

Fury gripped Baldock. He marched round the car, and stood alongside her.

"Back off," the would-be thief ordered.

He was dressed all in black, and wore a black balaclava to cover his face. The voice was gruff and angry, and in his hand the pistol shook as if he were as frightened as Lisa.

When she spoke, her voice was as shaky as the lad's hand.

"Just be calm. We only need to speak to you. No one's going to attack you."

Baldock scanned him from head to toe, and homed in on the stain at the young man's trouser cuff. Anger consumed him again. "Lipton, put that bloody thing down and take off that ridiculous headgear."

Even Lisa was surprised when Baldock called him by name. But not so surprised that when young Lipton glanced at Baldock, she didn't have time to kick the pistol from his hand. It spun away from him, clattered to the ground and broke into several pieces.

"Aw, now look. You've broke me gun."

"A toy," Lisa hissed and rounded on the teenager. "Peter, what are you playing at? And do as Raymond says, take that silly balaclava off."

Lipton did as he was told, and stared sulkily at the ground. "How'd you know it was me?"

"You still have that same gunge on your trousers," Baldock pointed to the white mess covering the youngster's trouser cuff. "Have you been doing some concreting or is your mother still working."

"It's not concrete. It's bread stuff. Dough."

"Doing your own baking, now?" Baldock took out his phone. "Right. Let's see how the police deal with you."

"No, Raymond." Lisa stayed him.

"He was about to steal my wheel... for the fourth time," Baldock protested. "And he aimed a weapon at you. All right, so it was a toy, but it's still threatening behaviour."

"Yes, it is, but let's see what we can get out of him, eh?" She faced the dejected young man. "Who did you sell the wheels to, Peter?"

"I'm not saying nothing."

"That's a double negative," Baldock pointed out, "and it means you are saying something."

Young Lipton frowned. "What?"

"Never mind the grammar lessons," Lisa insisted. "Peter, you have never been in trouble with the police, have you?"

He shook his head dumbly.

"Well now's as good a time as any to start your record," Baldock insisted, and again slid a finger over the phone's lock screen.

"No," Lisa insisted, and continued to pressure the young man. "But unless you tell us what's happening with these wheels, I will let Raymond ring the cops."

"It's not just me, you know," Lipton complained. "There's Josh as well. I don't see you pushing him about. It's cos he's black, isn't he?"

"No," Baldock replied. "It's because he's not here, you imbecile. Once we're through with you, we'll have a word with him, and Billy. Now where are the wheels going?"

When Lipton again refused to answer, Lisa said, "The only possibility is his father."

"Gary?" Baldock asked.

"Hmm, yes. I told you, he has his own car repair business. He could make money with those kind of wheels."

"Right. So we go see him."

"No." For the first time, young Lipton appeared worried. "You'll get me a pasting. It's not me dad."

"Then who?"

The answer was a long time coming, but at length, his eyes on the ground, lips pouting as if he were about to burst into tears, he said, "Ivan Haigh."

If the answer took Baldock by surprise, it astonished Lisa. "Haigh?"

The reply was a bare nod.

"And how much does he pay you for them?"

"Twenty dabs a wheel."

"Twenty pounds?" Baldock's fury began to rise again. "Those wheels are worth hundreds of pounds each."

"Well, you can buy 'em back off him for fifty each."

"You bloody little..." Baldock took a step forward and young Lipton backed off.

"It's pocket money, innit?" the teenager pleaded. "You don't know what it's like, you don't. Our old man never has any money, and even when he has, most of it goes paying me mam child support. He's always broke. Mam works all hours and she's still struggling to keep us. We do it for a bit of pocket money that's all. But you wouldn't know about that, would you? With your fancy cars, and your big bank accounts."

"As it happens, you're wrong, Lipton. I do know what it's like to be near penniless. I did three years of university scraping to make ends meet. My first job barely paid enough to cover the rent, but I still didn't go out stealing to supplement my income. Instead, I worked hard, bloody hard, and it paid off. But even if it hadn't, I still wouldn't have set about stealing car wheels." He looked down at the young man, his temper beginning to get the better of him again, but he knew Lisa would not allow him to report the matter. "Oh, go on. Get out of my sight."

Lipton appeared relieved, and grabbed the handlebars of his bicycle, but before he could get into the saddle, Lisa stayed him.

"Just a minute. Peter, the night Nate Perry went missing. He was supposed to meet you and Josh, wasn't he?"

Lipton shrugged. "Like I told plod, he never showed."

"Were you going out stealing wheels that night?"

No answer.

"Peter." There was a warning edge to Lisa's voice.

"All right, yes. There was this bloke up by the park. Had this fancy Beamer with good alloys, but no badge on 'em. Ivan would have paid us fifteen for each wheel without a badge. Me and Josh got to the park gates about nine, and Nate was supposed to be there with us. We gave him until half past, but he never showed. We went after the Beamer on our own, just me and Josh, but it's like the guy was waiting for us. He had this bleeding great mutt. A rottie. Jesus, it near jumped up like it was gonna us apart. Good job it were winter. We were both wearing thick clobber, so even if it'd got us, we'd have been okay."

"And you legged it?"

"We legged it."

"The man's name?" Baldock asked.

"How the hell do I know his name? We don't knock on his

door and ask who we're nicking 'em from, do we?"

Baldock could not fault the logic.

"Where does he live?" Lisa asked.

"Big house. Next to the church on Town Lane. Set back off the road."

"I know it," Lisa said.

Baldock could not place it. "Is it possible Nate went there alone? Casing the place?"

Lipton shrugged. "Coulda done. I dunno. All I know is Nate were supposed to meet us and he never showed."

With nothing more to press on the youngster, Lisa spoke again to Lipton. "All right, Peter, you can go, but bear in mind, we'll be talking to your parents about this."

"Aw, you can't do that—"

"You'd rather we spoke to the police?"

Silence.

"Go on, clear off." Baldock held up his phone. "Before I change my mind."

They watched him mount his bicycle and pedal off.

"We should have pushed him on this house where the alleged BMW was parked," Baldock said as he circled his car checking the wheels. "Nathan could have been killed there."

"I doubt it," Lisa said. "It's the vicarage, and Fletcher Tompkins, the present incumbent, owns both the Beamer and the Rottweiler."

"A vicar owning a Rottweiler? Unusual."

"Sue – the dog's name – is as gentle as a lamb, and if she came bounding towards Peter and Josh, it was probably because she wanted to play."

"A playful Rottweiler sounds to me like an investment banker digging out the Monopoly board." Baldock bent to examine the rear, offside wheel, where Lipton had been crouched when Lisa first confronted him. The socket wrench Lipton had been using was still attached to the locknut. As he removed it, Baldock said, "There doesn't appear to be any damage done. He never got the locking... hello... what's this."

He picked up a small, bubble-wrapped package, and held

it up for Lisa to see. Inside were two, pale blue pills.

"How did they get here?" she asked.

He held up the socket wrench. "They must have fallen out of his pocket when he pulled the wrench out. He's dealing."

"Not necessarily. He could have bought them for his own use."

"Fiagara?"

"You know they're Fiagara, do you?"

In deference to the thickness of the wrapping, Baldock nodded to his mother's house. "Let's go inside and find out. And if they are, you know where our next port of call is, don't you? His father."

They returned to the house and the kitchen, where he opened the tiny parcel, and found two, individually wrapped pills, both with the distinctive 'F' of Fiagara.

"There you are." Baldock was triumphant. "Lipton senior. I knew it. If anyone on this estate could be mixed up in drugs, it would be Gary Lipton."

Lisa was not so sure. "Gary is a scroat, all right, but he's never, to my knowledge, had anything to do with drugs."

"We'll soon find out."

"Not tonight, we won't," Lisa said.

"Strike while the iron is hot."

"Cliché," she chided him. "Writers don't deal in clichés, do they?"

"When they're apt."

"Yes, well, the real reason is it's Sunday night, and right now, Gary will be half pissed in the tap room of The Midden. We can leave him until tomorrow morning."

It made sense to Baldock. "All right. So what about Haigh and my wheels?"

"Now that," she said, "is the sensible option. We'll pay a call on Mr Haigh's back gates tonight. Say midnight-ish. After the pubs have cleared out."

***

The rear of the shops at the top of Midthorpe Avenue were accessed by a narrow path running off Midthorpe Mount, a street adjacent to Haigh's and at right angles to the Avenue.

With the time coming up to midnight, there were few people about, but Baldock, his prudence wrapped around him like a cocoon, worried about their forthcoming mission.

"It'll be all right, Raymond," Lisa assured him as he parked his car on Midthorpe Mount, near to the end of the path. "We're not doing anything illegal. Just taking a look. If Peter Lipton has it right, then you can confront Haigh in the morning."

"It would be just as simple to call the police."

"And give Ivan time to get rid of the evidence before they could come back with a warrant? Besides, they'd send Grunny, and it would take him until Wednesday to get here. Even then, he'd only insist on a cuppa and listen to Ivan's side of the story. No, Raymond, we need evidence." She tapped the shirt pocket in which he kept his phone. "As in pictures."

At the back of the shop, they were greeted with a ten-foot high wall, broken by double gates which were well over eight feet in height and locked solid on the other side.

"You do realise, if we're seen here, it isn't going to do our reputation much good," Baldock said as they chewed over the problem of how to get a look in the yard.

"How many more times, Raymond, it's not as if we're actually robbing the place, is it? Now come on. Let's get on with it."

With a cautionary glance up and down the road, Lisa stood alongside the gates, bent at the knee, her hands cupped.

Baldock shook his head. "No offence, Lisa, but you'll never hold my weight. I'll see if I can climb over."

"And you've just been moaning about the dangers of being nicked for breaking and entering." Now Lisa shook her head. "Tell you what, give me your phone, then you lift me up and I'll look over the gates."

He looked up at the gates, then down at Lisa, then up at the gates again, assessing how high he would have to lift her.

"Come on, Raymond. At this rate we'll get done for loitering, never mind thieving."

He bent at the knee, cupped his hands and she placed one foot in them. Gripping his shoulders, she hauled herself up and he lifted.

"A bit higher," she insisted, as she clung onto the top of the gate.

"I can't lift you any higher. Step onto my shoulders," he ordered.

Lisa did so, and Baldock immediately doubted the wisdom of his instructions as her shoes bit into his muscles. She told him she could see plenty of wheels and tyres of many shapes and sizes, and he automatically looked up and under her skirt. Even this late at night, he was treated to a glorious view of her holdups, the bare flesh above them and her tiny, white panties beyond.

"I can see a few wheels, but there's a big tarpaulin and I bet the best ones are hidden under that. What do your wheels look like?"

"Alloys..." he realised he was speaking straight up her skirt, and leaned back a little so he could speak to her instead. "Alloys."

"I know they're alloys, you banana. There's a couple of alloys here. How will I know which are yours?"

"Five spokes, Mercedes badge in the centre."

His brief description was followed by a long minute of silence during which his shoulders began to ache. Lisa, he reasoned, did not weigh much, but it was still more than his shoulders muscles, strong as they might be, were designed to carry.

He heard the false, electronically generated click of his phone's camera, and the flash bounced around the walls. "Don't know if I got ''em, but I've seen plenty to take him on."

He was relieved to hear it. "I've seen plenty, too?"

"Come again?"

"At this rate, I'm likely to."

"I can't hear you, Ray. Get me down."

It was a tricky proposition. It involved him taking hold of one ankle, and guiding her leg foot down to the level of his waist, where he could then grip her by the waist and let her down. Unfortunately, his head was still under her skirt as she came down, and by the time she was ready to hop to the ground, she was resting her hands on his head, and her skirt was raised so far that it would have had any passer-by reaching for a phone to either call the police or take incriminating pictures.

Smoothing down her skirt, Lisa made an effort to laugh it off. "Enjoy the view?"

"I, er…"

"Oh, don't be such a fuddy-duddy, Raymond. I don't have anything you haven't seen before. Probably on lots of women."

He grinned sheepishly and corrected her. "A few women. But it doesn't always come so attractively packaged."

"Ooh, a compliment. I'd better be careful or you might be after my body."

"I, er… Look, never mind the risqué repartee. Do we knock Haigh up?"

"I shouldn't. Leave it until tomorrow and we'll present him with the facts. You have a flashlight thingy that will show your registration on the inside of the wheel?"

"An ultraviolet lamp? Yes. It's in the car boot," he agreed.

"Then can challenge him tomorrow. First thing. Either that or you wait for me to finish work at half past four and we go together."

"No. I'll see him myself."

"Good. Let's go. What with you looking at my knickers, I'm feeling quite, er, anxious."

"Anxious as in…?"

"Up for it."

Chapter Thirteen

Baldock placed two tubes of mints on the counter. "No stamps, this time."

It was ten thirty, Monday morning, and after another night of intense activity with Lisa, Baldock was feeling tired, but in high spirits, actively anticipating the confrontations to come, which, he had no doubt, would put him where he believed he belonged: at the peak of the Midthorpe hierarchy.

It had been an interesting, and in many ways, exciting weekend. His attitude to Midthorpe had shifted some distance. He still regarded the tawdry little estate as a dump of the worst kind, but he had found some of its good heart, and he had found Lisa. He had to go home. He had commitments in Norwich which he could not avoid, but if their nascent relationship were to develop, he could foresee the day when a move back to north of England (but not Midthorpe) might be on the cards.

In the meantime, there were other matters to be handled and resolved, and it was no exaggeration to say that he was looking forward to putting one or two people in their place, beginning with Ivan Haigh.

He sat outside for ten minutes, watching the comings and goings of shoppers and when he was reasonably certain that there was no one in the place, he climbed out of his car, entered the shop, picked up the mints and placed them on the counter as Haigh emerged from his backroom.

Behind Haigh, the shelves of the e-cigarettes and SIM cards looked exactly as they had on Friday afternoon, as if none had been sold, and if that was an indication of the level of trade, Baldock felt he understood why Haigh might decide to supplement his income via stolen goods.

The shopkeeper, his ill-fitting, white smock swathing him

like a windbreak on a blustery beach, stared with great suspicion. "Two tubes of mints, sixty-five pee each, that's, one pound, thirty pee to you." He nodded at his cash register. "And I didn't need no machines or a pencil to add it up for me."

"Very good." Baldock took out his debit card. "Ten out of ten for mental arithmetic."

"Which is more than you get for learning." Haigh stared owlishly at the card. "Short memory, have we?"

"I'm sorry?"

"I don't take plastic for less than a tenner." Haigh glared even harder, but this time, straight into Baldock's eyes. "I told you that on Friday."

Baldock chuckled good-naturedly. "Sorry. My mistake. You're right. My memory is getting worse. I almost forgot, I want three alloy wheels for a Mercedes saloon."

He paid close attention to the shopkeeper's malleable features as they ran a gamut of emotions from alarm, puzzlement, irritation, and downright anger. "Are you just taking the mick or what?"

Baldock maintained his fake, amiable air. "No, no. I really do want three alloy wheels for a Mercedes. The three you bought from the toe rags who stole them from me in the first place will do fine."

Haigh backed off half a yard, and stopped when he hit the shelves behind him, and his display of e-cigs rocked precipitously. "Now look—"

"No. You look. At this." Baldock put his phone on the counter, displaying the photograph Lisa had taken the previous night. There were several wheels littering the back yard, and a huge lump under the tarpaulin Lisa had noticed, but one of those visible wheels bore the Mercedes logo. "Lisa Yeoman took that picture from your back gate last night."

In an obvious and desperate effort to avoid the issue, Haigh made an effort to go on the attack. "Lisa climbed over my back gates? That's burgalry, that is."

"The word is burglary, Haigh. Burglary, not burgalry. And you're wrong. She didn't break into your yard. She took this picture from the top of the gate, and that wheel is mine. I assume the other two are hidden under that tarpaulin."

"Yeah, well, it's still an invasion of privacy. I know. I've read all them books that whoisit, John Grisham, wrote."

"He's American and their laws are different to ours."

"I've watched Rumpole of the Bailey an'all."

"Twenty years out of date, Haigh. Now stop pratting about. You bought those wheels knowing them to be stolen."

"No, no. You're wrong." Sweat had begun to break out on Haigh's forehead and his eyes had a wild look about them. "They're mine. I used to have a Merc'."

Baldock dipped into the side pocket of his jacket, and came out with the ultraviolet light. "In that case, you won't mind if I take a look at them with this, will you? You see, Haigh, my registration is written on the inner rim, but it only shows up under this light. Now if it turns out that they are not my wheels, I will of course, apologise. But if they are mine… well, then it all depends on how reasonable you were willing to be."

Haigh swallowed hard. "Reasonable?"

Baldock turned up the pressure. "Do you know how much those wheels have cost me? In replacements, I mean? Over fifteen hundred pounds. I could quite legitimately sue you for that amount, plus damages for the inconvenience. And that's not to say what the police would make of this illegal trade. And when I say police, I don't mean Steven Grunwell. I mean the real police, like my good friend Detective Inspector Dawn Kramer."

He was satisfied to see near-panic setting in as Haigh stared wildly around, and he got the impression that the little shopkeeper was seeking some means of escape.

Baldock went on: "I work with the police a lot, you know. Research for my novels. I know that they regard receiving stolen goods as a worse offence than actually stealing them. Without people like you the thieves would have no market for their swag. Then there's the tax man and the VAT man. I daresay these transactions haven't gone through your books, and once HMRC learn of it, they'll estimate how much you've made illegally, and when they're estimating in their favour, they have this awful tendency towards generosity. On the whole, I'd guess you're staring bankruptcy in the face… once you get out of prison that is."

Haigh's body language, the sagging shoulders, the sagging face, the dulled eyes. Spelled defeat. "What do you want?"

"Well, first I want the wheels back. We can load them into the boot of my car right now."

"I have a shop…" He trailed off under Baldock's gimlet eye. "Right now. Course. No problem. Bring your car round the back, I'll open the gates."

"Then I want the names of the scroats who sold you the wheels—"

"No names. I'm a Midthorper, remember."

"I was about to say I want their names kept out of it," Baldock growled. "I know who they are, and I've been persuaded that they deserve a second chance. So if and when the pooh ever hits the fan, you don't know their names. Understood?"

"Gotcha. Anything else?"

"Yes. A couple of Fiagara pills."

For the first time, he came up against what appeared to be a genuine brick wall. "Ah. No. Wrong shop. Listen, Ballcock, I'm a bit iffy, granted, but I don't do those sweeties. Shippy is the man you need to see. That's where I get 'em."

Baldock decided that Haigh was too terrified to be telling anything but the truth. "In that case…" He placed a pound coin on the counter. "Just two packets of mints."

***

Baldock drove away from the rear of Haigh's with his three stolen wheels in the boot, and even though the entire fiasco exercise had cost him a considerable amount of money, he was nevertheless in high spirits.

Haigh had struggled to lift the three wheels into the car, but once it was done and Baldock had closed the boot, he made no complaint. "I take it we won't hear no more about this now?"

"To be perfectly frank, if I had my way, I'd have called the police, but Lisa persuaded me otherwise. Not for your sake, you understand, but for the little ratbags who were supplying you." With a broad smile of superiority, Baldock climbed behind the wheel of his car. "But don't forget, Haigh, this is a favour you'll owe me."

That final, parting line gave him the most pleasure. He had finally beaten one of Midthorpe's own and subdued him into submission. For one who had suffered so much at the hands of such people, it was a heady, intoxicating feeling, and he was sorely tempted to go straight to Gary Lipton's place of work and confront him, too; beat him down, have him begging for mercy.

"I shouldn't, Raymond," his mother suggested when he put the idea to her. "For a start off, you have no proof, only your suspicion, and secondly, Gary isn't Ivan Haigh. Gary would be just as likely to beat you to death."

"Oh come on Mother. That's stretching it a bit."

"You think so?" Tim asked. His voice had improved and continued to get stronger. "You're assuming Gary is mixed up in this Fiagara business, and we're all thinking that Nate Perry was into it, too. Someone killed Nate. If it was Gary, do you think he'd think twice about topping you?"

It made absolute sense, and was enough to put Baldock's plans on hold. "If all this is so, I don't really want to take Lisa anywhere near him, either."

Tim chuckled. "Don't you worry about our Lisa. She can deal with the Gary Liptons of this world."

"Would you not be better talking to the police?" Janet asked.

Baldock would have agreed in an instant. "The trouble is, Mother, that would mean letting them know about young Lipton and Josh Allen, and Lisa thinks they should be given another chance."

Janet sucked in her breath. "Ooh, it is awkward, isn't it?"

"Not from my point of view," her son argued. "Personally, I think prison would teach both Lipton and Allen a lesson they need to learn, but it seems I'm in a minority."

"I agree that it would work in some cases, Ray," Tim said, "But it can also go the other way, and that's the danger with Pete and Josh. Even your mum'll tell you, they're not bad kids, they just have a rough deal."

"Perfectly true, Raymond," his mother assured him. "Both those boys have helped us in the past, haven't they, Tim? They cut the hedges for me last summer."

"And they cleared all the rubbish from the garden during the winter," Tim said in support of Janet.

"For a price, obviously." Even to himself, Baldock sounded disparaging.

"Well, of course we paid them," his mother replied. "Twenty pounds, I gave them. They didn't ask for twenty. They asked if I'd pay five pounds for trimming the hedges, and I said yes. They did more, so I paid them more. They need a break, Raymond."

Baldock got to his feet. "Like I said, I'm in a minority." In a deliberate change of subject, he said, "I'd better get my case packed for the journey home."

"When are you going, Ray?" Tim asked.

"This evening. Or tomorrow morning at the latest. I've already scrubbed one publicity event. I daren't screw up the arrangements any further. I really have to be back in Norwich no later than tomorrow evening."

Having packed what he had at Lisa's, he went out to the car, retrieved his small case, then made his way up to his room, where he began to pack away the remainder of his clothing and toiletries. A glance at his travel clock said it was coming up to noon. Lisa would not finish work until four or four thirty (she wasn't sure). He had anything up to five hours to wait. But he didn't want to wait. He wanted to get on, close this business, and turn his thoughts to the rest of his life.

He spent the remainder of the day mooching around his mother's kitchen, half listening to the inane chatter between Janet and Tim, his eyes straying constantly to the clock, while his laptop stood open on the table, a journal open where he made notes on the remarkable weekend or pottered with half-formed ideas for a new series of novels, a senior detective from a humble background, such as his, still working amongst what he described as the detritus of society.

His attention wandered frequently, homing in on the confrontation to come, running through the various, possible scenarios. Lipton, he would agree, was an impatient idiot, only too willing to bring his fists into play when challenged, but was he truly dangerous? If, as seemed likely, Nathan Perry (after speaking to Hardwick, Baldock was certain the body in the woods was young Perry) was shot to death, did that mean Lipton would bring a shotgun to bear on him and Lisa? The thought of leading her into such danger filled him with trepidation, but curiously, his own safety never occurred to him. His rage at the man who had bullied him so much for so long, precluded any such thoughts. He was out to teach Lipton a lesson he should have learned years ago, and coincidentally lock him away for life.

To his surprise, Lisa turned up before four o'clock.

"My last client cancelled." She accepted a beaker of tea from Janet. "I've lost fifty pounds, but at least I get off early."

"Fifty pounds? I thought you worked for the NHS," Baldock objected.

"No. I'm contracted to the NHS, but I work for myself. Remember? I told you about it on Friday night."

Baldock could not recall her saying anything of the kind on Friday night, but he chose not to argue. Lisa hurriedly drank her tea, and passing the cup to Janet, said, "Right. Let's go see what Gary has to say for himself, eh?"

Baldock was ahead of her. Having been keyed up with the prospect for much of the day, he did not even open the door to let her out first, but instead, strode through and let her follow.

Lisa directed him, although he did not need directions, through the streets off Midthorpe Walk, until they pulled up outside one of a long row of town houses on Midthorpe Crescent. Ringing the doorbell produced no answer.

"Gary lives on his own," Lisa said. "Has done ever since Annette left him. Ten to one he'll be in his workshop."

"You're sure he won't be in the public bar of The Midden?"

"At half past four on a Monday afternoon? Even Gary needs some time away from the beer, so he can earn the money to spend in The Midden. Let's try his place. It's one of the industrial units off Tansey Lane. You remember them?"

"My father said they were allotments and piggeries when he was a kid."

Tansey Lane ran past the estate at the bottom off Midthorpe Avenue. A main road running west from the Wakefield area to the M62 at Tingley, it had always been noted for the open fields around it.

Baldock turned right onto the Lane from Midthorpe Avenue, drove for about100 yards, and then turned left into a narrow track. 'Narrow' was comparative, he decided as they drove slowly down the dirt road past a hotchpotch of small industrial units, and larger, open yards; it was nowhere near as wide as the main road, but it was still broad enough to allow lorries the access they needed.

With the shed and workshops on the left, a large breakers' yard stood on the right, and just past it, was a similar yard for salvaging and recycling 45-gallon drums.

Further along, they passed a pallet yard with an old, burnt out skip in front of the gates.

"A regular call for the Fire Service," Lisa told Baldock. "Gary's place is near the bottom. Close to the old railway line."

Baldock nodded and juggled his car from one side to the other, slaloming his way down in an effort to avoid the worst of the potholes. He spotted Terry Hardwick climbing out of his car and unlocking the door of one shed, but he did not comment. He was too keyed up with the coming confrontation.

Lipton had the double doors of his small workshop open to let in some of the summer warmth and sun. It also helped rid the place of the smell of paint which he was applying to a light blue, 1983 Ford Escort.

As they climbed out of the Mercedes, he removed his face mask, and greeted them with a contemptuous snarl.

"What do you want, Ballcock? Another thumping?"

"After the other night, I should have thought you were the one to worry, Lipton."

"Lucky punch." Lipton put down his spray gun. "Wanna try again?"

"Don't be absurd." Baldock would not be drawn and he would not back down. "I'm looking for someone manufacturing drugs which are poisonous. And off hand, I'd say I've found him." He gestured at the car and said to Lisa. "Viagra blue. Now we know what poisoned your father."

Lisa did not have time to answer before Lipton responded. "I don't know what you're talking about, but if you accuse me again you'll need a coat of pink paint to cover the bruises."

Lipton stepped forward, fists clenched, Baldock prepared to meet him and Lisa inserted herself between them.

"Stop it. Both of you. Just stop it." She glared from one to the other. "Do you know how evenly matched you are?"

Baldock took instant offence and so too did Lipton judging by the look on his face.

"You, Raymond, are intellectually superior, and you Gary, are physically superior. Unfortunately for both of you, I'm your intellectual match, Raymond, and your physical match, Gary. Now knock it off or I'll deck the pair of you."

She allowed them a moment to calm down.

"Now, Gary. Are you making and selling fake pills?"

"What?" He was astounded. "For f… for god's sake, Lisa, you know me. I've been hooky most of me life, but I've never done drugs. I don't use 'em, I don't sell 'em, I don't care for 'em and I don't have nowt to do with 'em."

"You've obviously had the same English training as your son, too," Baldock snapped. "And talking of your son, did you know he's dealing in drugs… well, fake pills at the very least."

"Yes."

Baldock appealed to Lisa. "You see? Persistent denial. I told you we should have called... what did you say?"

Lipton opened the driver's door of the car he was working on, and squatted on the seat, his feet on the dirty floor, one elbow resting on his knee, the hand cupping his jaw. He looked downtrodden and beaten. "He's been at it a year. When I pushed him on it, he said it wasn't drugs, it was Viagra stuff. I warned him to knock it off. He wouldn't. I keep asking who he's working for and he won't tell me." Lipton appealed to Lisa, not Baldock. "He lives with Annette, and I don't have any control over him. Not since I had to move out. I could leather his arse, but it wouldn't make any difference. He'd only have me walled up for assault."

Baldock sneered. "It never occurred to you to report it to the police?"

"Don't be soft, Ballcock. You know the unwritten code on Midthorpe. You never grass anyone. Especially not your own. Listen, I know you can't stand the sight of me. Well, that's fair enough. If truth be told, I worship the ground you've got coming to you, but do you think I don't want better for my lad? Eh? You think I don't want to see him with money like what you've got? Well I would. He's a good lad, and I don't care what anyone says, he's bright, he's smart. Not just street smart, but book smart. Like you. Everyone says so. He can do better for himself than I ever did, and if I could just find out who's paying him, I'd get him out of it, cos I'd chase him so far from this estate our Pete'd never see him again, let alone sell his 'toffees' as they call 'em."

Silence fell for a moment. Baldock was both amazed and puzzled by this new Gary Lipton, the caring parent.

Lisa spoke first. "It might interest you to know, Gary, that Peter attacked us yesterday. He was trying to steal another of Raymond's wheels. He's already had three. When I confronted him, he pulled a gun on us."

Lipton's mouth fell open. "A gun?"

"It was a toy, and it got broke," Lisa assured him. "Gary, one of those toffees, as you call them, sent my father to A & E on Friday night. Other pills sent Shippy, John Taplin, and

Malcolm Norris to hospital. Whatever Peter is pushing, they're not harmless sweets."

With the feeling that he should add something, Baldock said, "And according to our information, they're not Viagra substitutes, either. In fact they do nothing but poison the victim."

The colour returned to Lipton's face and continued through the spectrum until it was the rose red of fury. "I'll kill him."

"Now, Gary—"

"No way, Lisa. Our Peter has done well. At his age, I'd already been inside once, but he's never been in trouble with the filth. Well, I'll make sure he doesn't get in trouble with 'em. I'll scare the living daylights out of him. Just leave it with me. And I'll tell you summat else; if I find whoever's selling them to our Pete first, there won't be anything left for the law."

Chapter Fourteen

The short journey from Tansey Lane back to Janet's was conducted in near silence. Lisa made the occasional comment on the weather or the state of the roads, Baldock responded with non-committal grunts.

Lisa, he guessed – he *hoped* – was concerned with his departure and if truth be told, it was on his mind, too, but as he drove along Midthorpe Avenue, he was more centred on the revelation of Gary Lipton.

The man had loomed large in Baldock's memory for the last two decades and longer, and Baldock the novelist could have cast him in many roles: mobster, psychopath, serial killer, bank robber. But never would it have occurred to him to see Lipton as the concerned father.

And it was genuine, not an affectation. Seated in the car, the way his shoulders had slumped, the way the disappointment, the worry had been etched into his face would have taken years of drama training for it to be anything but real. Gary Lipton was not that good an actor. He really cared about his son, and wanted the boy to have a better life than he had.

Making the right turn into Midthorpe Walk, it dawned on Baldock that the underlying foundations of his own drive and determination were suffering a tectonic shift. The hatred of this estate and the people who inhabited it, which had long spurred the flames of his motivation, was not quite the bedrock he had built upon.

He dare not broach the subject with Lisa. Her opinion of Midthorpe was as coloured as his, albeit of a lighter shade, and he knew perfectly well what her response would be: 'I told you so'.

And yet, he recognised that Lisa was central to this change in attitude. The weekend had been one of raw and exciting sex, the realisation of a desire that was two decades old for both of them. But was it more than that? It was a learning curve, and something else, but was that something the first spark of love? It seemed unlikely to Baldock, but that was because the concept of a loving relationship had never dawned on his consciousness in his entire life. Glancing across at Lisa as he turned into the Terrace towards his mother's, he knew she would think differently. She had had relationships; proper relationships based not purely on sex. They had failed, but that did not necessarily mean she had given up on the matter.

Pulling up, killing the engine and applying the parking brake, he wondered best how to broach the subject.

"Lisa—"

"Raymond—"

A short silence followed by chuckles.

"Midthorpe is going to come between us, isn't it?" Lisa asked.

He nodded. "To some degree."

"Is that what you were going to say?"

"I was going to ask whether there is an 'us' for Midthorpe to come between. Or has it just been, er, sex?"

"I think it's more than that, but we need time to be sure, and that would be tough considering you live in Norwich and I live here. Long distance relationships are difficult to handle."

"I can imagine." He smiled ruefully. "I'm not good on relationships, long distance or otherwise. I've never had one that lasted longer than a month or two."

"And I don't suppose there's a chance of you moving back to Midthorpe?"

"Short of absolute bankruptcy and destitution causing me to throw myself on my mother's mercy, no."

"How about Leeds in general?" Lisa began to warm to her theme, half turning in her seat so she could face him. "You see, Raymond, I love my job, and it's here, on this estate, and

I have to live within travelling distance. Correct me if I'm wrong, but you could live wherever you wished."

"I could, and right now, I like Wroxham." He drummed his fingers on the steering wheel. "I could come up to Leeds more often; say once a month. Just until we see where, if anywhere, we're going."

She nodded. "And I suppose I could come down to Norfolk now and then."

He nodded, deciding that he had not expected anything more. "I'd better get my gear packed and ready for the off."

"You're leaving tonight?"

"That's the plan."

Her face fell.

"I could leave early in the morning, I suppose," he told her, and her face brightened again.

"One last night of wild passion?" She laughed. "Enough to last a month or two?"

"Why not?"

They climbed out of the car and ambled into his mother's kitchen, where they found both Janet and Tim watching the late afternoon news on the BBC.

While Lisa gave them a rundown on what had happened with Gary Lipton, Baldock took his small case out to the car and dropped it into the boot. It was a tight squeeze, but the three wheels filling most of the available space, pleased him, and the iniquities of wriggling one small piece of baggage into the remaining space did not detract from that pleasure.

With that done, he checked the interior of the car to ensure Lisa had not left anything behind, then spent a few moments sat in the passenger seat, his legs hanging out of the car, the way Lipton had done.

Even with the door open, the car was filled with her scent, invoking a plethora of mental images from the last few days. Happy, serious, light-hearted, arousing, contented; a range of emotions, most of which he was unfamiliar with in such numbers and intensity. Confusion assailed him. He was supposed to leave in the next hour, but he knew he would not. He knew he would go for that 'one last night of wild passion' as Lisa had described it.

And yet, he wanted to go home, get away from this area which had given him so much grief throughout his entire life. But at the same time, he wanted to be near to Lisa, to talk, listen, laugh, even cry with her, or simply hold her. His confused feelings were an internalised, alien landscape, and he did not know what to do about them.

The strong sunshine beamed into the car, warming and brightening everything, and it seemed to be saying to him, 'Get the pole out of your backside, Baldock, and learn to enjoy life.'

How? He did not know. Whenever he tried, his natural surliness would show through. Only with Lisa could he even begin to understand the concept, but soon Lisa would be on his list of once-a-month contacts...

"Raymond. Quick. It's Inspector Kramer."

His mother's voice reached him from her front door where she was waving frantically at him.

He climbed out of the car and hurried back to the house.

"It's about Nathan," Janet urged, "And that Inspector Kramer is due to make a statement."

The national news had finished and as Baldock joined them in the kitchen, the local news cut from the studio to Kramer standing outside the police station delivering a prepared statement.

"We can confirm that the body discovered in Midthorpe Woods yesterday, is that of Nathan Perry, who disappeared from his Midthorpe home early in the New Year. Up until now, we have refused to comment upon the cause of death, but forensics analysis has confirmed that damage to the ribs and pelvic area, indicate that Nathan was shot at close range by a 12-gauge shotgun. Our inquiries are now centred upon speaking to those people known to Nathan who are licensed for such firearms."

Baldock's face drained. "Oh my God. I know who it is."

While the gaggle of reporters pressed Kramer for more information, Lisa, Janet and Tim turned to face Baldock.

"What?" Lisa demanded.

"It's so bloody obvious when you think about it, too."

"Raymond, what are you talking about?"

He shook himself out of his stupor. "Mother, get on to Inspector Kramer. Tell her I know who it is, and ask her to meet us at the industrial units off Tansey Lane."

"Raymond," Lisa said, "it is not Gary Lipton."

"I know it isn't," he said, to her surprise. "I don't know which unit it is, Mother, but tell Kramer to look for my car. It'll be parked nearby. Lisa, I don't like asking you along because it could be dangerous, but I'll need another witness."

"I'll come," Tim volunteered and got to his feet.

"No you won't, Dad." Lisa stayed him and prepared to leave with Baldock. "You're not well enough for anything like this. But I am and I wouldn't miss it." She smiled aggressively at Baldock. "Besides, Raymond, you might need some protection."

***

Nothing seemed to have changed in the tiny industrial estate, and the car was still parked outside the shed where Baldock had first seen it. Parking his Mercedes across the back of it to prevent a getaway, he looked past Lisa and at the workshop. The roller shutter was down, and the access door alongside it was closed.

"How can you be so sure, Raymond?"

"Inspector Kramer said they've just confirmed that the murder weapon was a shotgun. No one knew before now, but he knew yesterday."

"The cops could have mentioned it to the Perrys."

"But he wasn't sat with the Perrys. He was outside, keeping out of it. He even said so." Baldock prepared to get out. "It's him. He may be armed, so you wait here while I confront him."

"And leave you as dead as Nathan?" Lisa opened her door. "Not likely."

They walked up the slight rise and tested the access door. Locked.

Baldock pressed his ear to it and listened. From inside, he could hear the sound of machinery running and the rhubarb mutter of low voices. It could have been the TV or a small group of men talking.

Leaving the door, Baldock rattled the shutter.

A moment later, the side door opened and Josh Allen appeared.

"Whaddya want?"

"Someone who knows how to speak English." Pushing the young man out of the way, Baldock barged past into the workshop.

Josh complained loudly, Lisa, too, pushed him aside and followed Baldock, while Josh brought up the rear and closed the door behind him.

Workshop was a misnomer. It was more like a small bakery, but what they were producing was not bread. A large mixer chugged and turned slowly, its beaters turning a mass of doughy substance into a paste. Beyond it, a small machine was pressing pills, presumably from similar paste which had been allowed to set, and dropping them into a stainless steel collection plate. On a flat, spotlessly clean bench, a large roll of bubblewrap was set on a roller, with cutting blades to trim to size. Peter Lipton was working on it, cutting and using small pieces to wrap up individual pills.

In another corner was a portable TV, showing the local BBC weather forecast, and next to it was a tall, broad storage cupboard, where Hardwick was pottering.

He turned to greet them cheerfully, "Ah. Baldock and the lovely Lisa Yeoman. I've been expecting you."

Baldock could not hide his surprise. "You have?"

Hardwick closed the cupboard door and faced them. "Well, either you or the police. Ever since I saw that news bulletin." He waved at the TV and grinned. "I assume that's what tipped you off."

Baldock nodded. "When I spoke to you at the Perrys' place, you knew about the shotgun, yet the police hadn't told anyone. Not even the Perrys. There was only one way you could have known, and that was because you shot the boy."

"And if I don't own a shotgun? What then of your theory?"

"Then you must have witnessed it, which means you know who did it." Baldock's eyes passed over Josh and Peter. "We've called the police, naturally."

"I imagine you have. And you're going to look a proper tit when they learn you're wasting their time." Hardwick laughed. "Still, you're both Midthorpers, even if you have been educated a bit beyond your station, and the cops are used to dealing with the scum from this estate."

"Scum like Peter and Josh?" Lisa demanded. "And Nathan?"

If he was at all concerned, Hardwick did not show it. "You see, Lisa, Peter, Josh and Nate were all tarred with that same Midthorpe brush. What chance do they have of making their way in the world? None."

"I did all right," Baldock declared. "So did Lisa. And I'm sure we're not the only two."

"You were lucky, Baldock. You've said so yourself in many an interview. Lisa was... well, not exactly lucky, but clever enough to get out, then stupid enough to come back. Just like you." Hardwick shrugged. "What can I say? You're Midthorpers. Midthorpe and stupidity are familiar bedfellows."

Baldock sighed. "English teachers. Who'd have them? If you mean Midthorpe and stupidity go together, then say so, Hardwick. Don't dress it up in fancy language or you'll never make a novelist."

This provoked more laughter from the teacher. "I don't want to be a novelist. I just want to go through life with enough money to make sure I can pay my bills, and have enough left to enjoy myself."

"By dealing in drugs?"

Hardwick wagged a disapproving finger at Lisa, and then waved at the pills. "These are not drugs, Ms Yeoman. They are sweeties. Isn't that right, Peter? Josh?"

Grinning broadly, the two youngsters nodded.

Lisa's anger rose. "One of those sweeties put my father

and three other men in hospital."

Her announcement wiped the smiles from the teenagers' faces.

Hardwick was insistent. "They contain nothing but flour, water, milk, baking soda, a lot of chalk and some sugar, and when it's ready, edible dye to make sure it turns the correct colour of blue. Absolutely nothing that would do you any harm."

With an effort at nonchalance, Baldock said, "Oh I don't know. The sugar would help put on a bit of weight.

Hardwick laughed. "They're placebos. A man can't get a hard on, give him a blue pill which he is convinced is a Viagra substitute, and suddenly he can take his missus to heaven. Where's the harm in that?"

"The batch in question contained drain cleaner," Baldock said. "What were you trying to do? Spice up the taste? Help them fight off potential sexually transmitted infection by killing germs inside the vagina?"

For the first time, the humour faded from Hardwick's features. "Yes, it was a bit of a downer, wasn't it? Tough luck that it was your dad who caught the first one, too, Lisa. It was Nathan's fault. He came here, one night in January, there was a bit of an argument, and he deliberately spilled a bottle of drain cleaner into the mixer. We were weeks sorting it out and I thought we'd got rid of it all. Must have been a trace left over in one or other of the ingredients." He smiled broadly. "Still, it's all over now, isn't it, and everyone is fine."

"Except Nathan," Lisa pointed out. "That night in January, when there was 'a bit of an argument', you shot him, didn't you? One of you three took a shotgun and dealt with him."

"No way," Peter Lipton said. "Me and Josh weren't even here, were we, Josh?"

"We was casing that house near the park," Josh confirmed. "We saw Terry going in the park, but we didn't hang about. Later, he told us Nate had got chuffed off with flogging fake pills and wanted the real thing, so he took off. Innat right, Terry?"

"Dead right, Josh."

Baldock was not listening. He was looking past Hardwick into the cupboard where he was sure he could see...

"So you didn't use that shotgun on him?"

They all fell silent, only the gentle rumbling of the mixer and the rattle of pills falling from the press into the collection tray to disturb the air.

Hardwick pulled on a pair of washing up gloves, turned into this cupboard and came out with the weapon.

Even the two teenagers were surprised and nervous.

"Hey up, Terry—" Peter began, only to be cut off by his teacher.

"It's all right, Peter," Hardwick assured him, and offered the gun. "Take it, break it. It's not loaded.

"Peter don't," Baldock warned. "You'll get your prints all over it."

Peter hesitated, but Hardwick became more assertive. "Take it, Peter. Or you'll join Nate."

The young man's face became a mixture of fear and resentment. He reached out a tentative hand and took both barrels.

"Now break it," Hardwick ordered.

Peter swung the gun round, taking hold of the stock, and broke the barrels. His eyes widened in horror. "You said it wasn't loaded and it is."

Baldock fumed. "You really are as gormless as your father, aren't you? Of course it's loaded. He's going to kill Lisa and me, the way he murdered Nathan. But he's wearing kitchen gloves, you're not. Your prints are all over that gun, so if anyone gets collared, it will be you, not him. When he has that hold over you, he will insist that you and Josh help him get rid of our bodies, and when that happens, Peter, you'll be in too deep to get out. If you're ever arrested, he'll claim that you forced him to help you, not the other way round, and he'll get just a few years, or maybe even probation. He could even get away with it altogether, while you two serve life sentences for crimes he committed."

Hardwick held out his hand for the gun, and Peter, still

terrified into a near-stupor, handed it back. Hardwick snapped the barrels shut and levelled the gun at the space between Baldock and Lisa.

"You, know, Baldock, you should stick to writing crime stories, not trying to investigate them for real. The scenario you just came up with could have come out of one of your Headingley novels… and it's bang on the mark."

"The police will be on their way," Lisa reminded him.

"I doubt it. But even if they are, so what? By the time they get here you two will be dead and in the boot of Baldock's car, which, obviously, will have been moved."

"With all those stolen wheels in the boot, you'll be hard pressed to get one body in, never mind two."

Both Hardwick and Lisa ignored Baldock's remark.

"This is just what you did with Nate, isn't it?"

"Well, to be honest, no. Nate was more of an accident than murder. He came here shouting the odds. He'd sold some fake Ecstasy to one of his customers, and the guy came back threatening and demanding either the real thing or his money back. Nate wanted the real McCoy, but I couldn't do that. I didn't have any. We argued, he threw the bloody drain cleaner in the mixer, and I got the gun out, just to calm him down. He grabbed the barrels and pulled me towards him, my finger was on the trigger and the gun went off. I never told these two, but I spent most of that night cleaning up in here and burying Nate in Virgin's Valley, where he would still be if you two hadn't fancied a legover yesterday."

Hardwick appeared to relax but for all that, the gun did not waiver.

"It's a funny thing about killing, you know. The first time, it's terrible. You're scared someone may have witnessed it, you want to cover it up but you're not sure how. That happened to me with a drug dealer outside Huddersfield ten, maybe fifteen years ago, and I managed to plant enough evidence on one of his scum friends to get away with it. But it's like getting between your girlfriend's legs. After the first time, you know a bit more about it and the more you do it, the better you get at it. Nate was the third man I'd killed, and even though his death was accidental, dealing with it was no worse than hard work. With you two, it'll be even easier." He leered at Lisa. "But I must admit, when it comes to you, Lisa, I'd rather be rogering than shooting."

She was about to respond, but Peter got there first. "Hang on, you're saying you shot Nate, and you knew all this time that he hadn't done a runner?"

Hardwick chuckled and said to Baldock, "See. Midthorper. Thick as a brick." Half turning he spoke to Peter. "Yes, I killed Nate, and in a minute or two, you're going to watch me kill these two, then help me get rid of them. Either that, or you go with them, and trust me if Josh watches me kill them and you, he'll be ready to help to save his own slimy, black skin."

Baldock took advantage of the distraction to scoop up a handful of the doughy paste from the mixer. It was not yet ready and still felt wet and loose in his hand.

"A racist too?" Lisa snapped. "How the hell did you ever get into teaching?"

Hardwick laughed and turned the gun back on them. "By feeding the interview panel the bull-poop they wanted to hear."

"You should fry in hell."

"I may, but it's not something either of you will be here to see." Hardwick raised the shotgun and took aim.

Baldock said a silent prayer. He had no idea whether what he was about to do would work, but given the choice between trying and dying, he knew which was preferable.

His luck was in when Peter tried to intervene. "Terry, no. You can't do this."

The gun swung to Hardwick's right, Baldock's left. "Shut up, you little tosser, or you go with them.

The gun began to arc back, and Baldock moved.

He spun to his right, his left arm coming round, and launched the handful of paste at Hardwick. At the same time, he pushed Lisa away, and then dropped to the floor. Peter and Josh also dropped.

The paste hit Hardwick in the face, the gun boomed in the

small, enclosed space. Baldock's left arm, having delivered the makeshift missile, was already raised, and as he fell, he felt the sting of shot hitting in several places around his forearm and bicep.

As she hit the floor, Lisa snatched up a short, metal shovel, presumably used for dropping flour into the mixer. Hardwick struggled to see through the goo on his face, and the shotgun waved erratically here and there, she rammed the metal edge into the barrels. It veered to Baldock's left, Hardwick's right, and the second barrel discharged harmlessly into the shed wall. Not to be outdone, Peter snatched the shotgun away from Hardwick, and Josh fell on the man pinning him to the floor.

To Baldock's pained surprise, Hardwick threw Josh off and struggled to his knees, snatching up the shovel Lisa had used. He brought it up and round, making to bring it down on her like a club, but his jaw presented itself to her and her fist connected with it. Hardwick paused for a moment as if trying to decide what he should do next then let the shovel fall and dropped flat on his face.

Ensuring he was out cold, Lisa then attended to Baldock. "My God, I've never been so scared." She checked his wounds.

"I thought shotgun pellets at such close range would do more damage." Baldock winced. "And hurt more."

She looked up. It's not shot, Raymond, it's glass." She pointed up at the ceiling strip which had taken the first shot and showered them with fragments. "I'm sure you'll live, but we need to get those cuts treated." She faced Peter and Josh. "Thank you, lads. What you've just done should save you from prison."

"We need to get the police out," Baldock insisted through gritted teeth. Digging into his pocket, he came out with his mobile.

"That was either incredibly brave or incredibly stupid, Raymond."

"It was neither," he insisted as he punched in Kramer's number. "It was desperate. The only option I had."

Chapter Fifteen

Baldock found Lipton working in his garage on his old car.

It had been a trying eighteen hours since the events in Hardwick's workshop. Lisa's assessment of his trivial wounds was correct. When the paste hit Hardwick in the face, his automatic reaction was to turn away, and in doing so, he had raised the barrel to the point where it missed the already falling Baldock and Lisa, and instead hit the strip lighting, which shattered. As Lisa said, it was glass shards which hit Baldock's arm, and then dropped onto the floor, lending the impression that he had absorbed some of the pellets.

Attended by paramedics, who cleaned and dressed the cuts and ordered him to see his GP for a tetanus shot and a possible course of antibiotics, he and Lisa gave separate statements to the police, and Hardwick accused them both of lying.

"The workshop is theirs," he insisted.

"And I commute daily from Norwich, don't I?" Baldock had sneered by return.

After a disturbed night consisting of more sex and little sleep, Baldock and Lisa arrived at his mother's to find Inspector Kramer in the kitchen yet again. She was talking to Janet and Tim, and the news was not good.

"It's his word against yours, Mr Baldock... well yours and yours, Ms Yeoman. Peter Lipton and Josh Allen have both given statements and they say they only arrived after the events. The only fingerprints we found on the weapon were young Lipton's and he says it's because he picked it up to move it to safety, away from all of you. When we confronted Hardwick with that, he changed his story slightly. He insists the workshop is nothing to do with him and that you got him there under false pretences so you could lay the blame on him. He maintains that the place is yours, Mr Baldock, and that Ms Yeoman runs it with Peter Lipton and Josh Allen helping. Neither Peter nor Josh will say anything on that matter."

"Check who owns the place," Baldock insisted.

"We did. It's rented from the Council and the lessee is a company named Fiagara Nights. When we checked, the company, naturally, doesn't exist, and it seems as if the rent is paid, in cash, every month."

"And no one at the Council found that odd?" Baldock demanded.

"No. They just assumed it was a cottage industry and that the proprietor was being very honest. We're currently looking into CCTV coverage of the local rent office to see if there's any clue as to who might have been paying the money over. We will get him, and when we do, we can pin the fake drugs on him. We've also taken the shotgun, which he insists is yours, Ms Yeoman, and we're hoping we can find some trace, no matter how tiny, to link it to the murder of Nathan Perry."

"Ballistics?" Lisa asked.

"No ballistic fingerprinting with shotgun cartridges," Baldock explained before Kramer could answer.

Determined not to be outdone, the inspector added, "It's because the shot is held in a plastic case and most of it doesn't touch the gun barrel. You can try to match firing pin imprints, but to do that we'd need the cartridge case of the shot that killed Nathan and we don't have it."

"So Hardwick is going to get away with it?" Lisa demanded.

"Not necessarily, but it's not so clear cut, either. That gun is unlicensed, so theoretically, it could belong to any of you. We need testimony from both Lipton and Allen to corroborate everything, but they're saying nothing because they're scared they're facing jail."

After scolding them for not calling the police, and then thanking them for their efforts, Kramer left, and Lisa came up with her idea. Baldock was against it, but she insisted.

Worse, when he suggested they get in his car and go together, she could not.

"I have a meeting, Raymond, and time is getting on. Speak to Gary yourself and if you don't get anywhere, I'll go after work."

The result was that he was now confronted with the obnoxious Lipton and neither of them were in the best of moods.

"Not got your knight in shining armour, Ballcock. Maybe we should settle outstanding business."

"Tell me, Lipton, were you born an idiot or was it one of those classes I missed at Midthorpe Primary?"

"You're asking for a busted arm to go with the one you've already got."

"Oh shut up, you fool, and for once in your life, listen."

"Just bugger off, Ballcock. Now. While you can still walk."

With a sigh, Baldock ignored the threat and pressed on. "The police arrested Terry Hardwick last night. He's the one who's been using your boy and Josh Allen to distribute thee fake drugs."

The news stopped Lipton in his tracks. "Has he now? Wait while he gets out."

"If you listen to me, he won't get out. He also murdered Nate Perry, but the law doesn't have enough evidence to charge him because your boy and Josh Allen will not tell them what really happened. If someone doesn't come forward, he'll get away with it. Now listen carefully, Lipton. Your son, Peter and Josh were there last night and they heard Hardwick confess to murdering Nathan Perry. You have to persuade Peter to tell the police everything, and let him persuade Josh to do the same."

"Oh yeah," Lipton sneered. "And Pete and Josh go down for dealing drugs. It's not gonna happen."

"Yes it is, and I'll tell you why. They were never selling drugs. Those pills had no active ingredients. It's a technicality, but we may be able to get them off with it. They will face charges, but Lisa has persuaded me that they should come clean, tell the law everything and make sure Hardwick answers for killing Nate Perry."

"My lad will still go down," Lipton protested. "It's what I've been trying to avoid."

"Correct. Personally, I think prison is the best place for him… the best place for anyone from Midthorpe, but Lisa doesn't agree. She is willing to go to court and testify on Peter's behalf… and Josh's of course. I'm on my way back to Norwich this afternoon, but I have already agreed to submit written testimony to Peter's impeccable past, and Josh's, and I'm also willing to perjure myself by telling the courts how hard you've worked to ensure he doesn't get into trouble." He paused to let Lipton take in the offer. "Lisa's word counts for a lot in this part of the world. Mine counts for very little, but I am a respected member of the literary community and that alone will compel the courts to take my testimony into account. Peter and Josh will still end up in court, but between us we should be able to keep them out of prison."

Lipton considered the offer for a long moment. "All right. Thanks, Ballcock. I'll talk to him. Get him to see sense." He smiled, showing tobacco-stained teeth. "Maybe you're not such a bad pain in the arse after all."

"Which is more than I would be prepared to say about you. And don't thank me. It was Lisa's idea and she persuaded me, against my better judgement, to go along with it."

"Well, tell her thanks. No, better yet, tell her if she needs another good seeing to, she knows where to find me."

Baldock, about to leave. Stopped, turned and stared. "What?"

Lipton grinned. "Oh, sorry, didn't she tell you about me and her? It was after you cleared off to Ferrybridge or wherever. Like dynamite we were."

***

Lisa watched as Baldock spoke to Janet. "Right, Mother. I'm away. I'll ring when I get home."

With Tim also stood by, Janet made a final plea to her son. "Must you go, Raymond? I don't like the thought of you driving all that way with a damaged arm."

"A few cuts and bruises. They'll soon heal."

With her meeting over, Lisa had cried off for an hour to be at Janet's to see Baldock off. Now she pleaded with him. "Why not say a while longer? As people find out what you did, I'm sure their attitude to you will change."

He turned her down right away. "I don't have bosses hanging over me, telling me to get on with my job, but I still have a job to do and responsibilities which go with it. I can't fulfil those here. I'm going home."

He pecked his mother on the cheek and marched out of the door. Lisa followed.

"What's wrong, Raymond?" she asked as he opened the drivers' door.

"Why should there be anything wrong?" He climbed behind the wheel.

Lisa leaned into the window as he let it down. "Well, you've been, I dunno, distant since I got here. Is it because I couldn't go to Lipton's with you? Did he hassle you or something? Only I did explain. I had no choice. I had to be at that meeting."

He fired the engine and roughly closed the door past her. "I said, I don't have bosses hanging over me, but you do, and you have to do what you have to do."

Lisa sighed. "Raymond, take a leaf from your own book. Tell it like it is."

He snapped the parking brake off and held the car on the footbrake. "All right." He glared up. "I know about you and Lipton."

Lisa had to back off quickly as he released the brake and hit the gas.

"Raymond," she called out after the disappearing car. "Wait. Ray. Please listen to me…"

THE END

The Midthorpe Murder Mystery series:
A Case of Missing on Midthorpe
A Case of Bloodshed in Benidorm

The STAC Mystery series:
The Filey Connection
The I-Spy Murders
A Halloween Homicide
A Murder for Christmas
Murder at the Murder Mystery Weekend
My Deadly Valentine
The Chocolate Egg Murders
The Summer Wedding Murder
Costa del Murder
Christmas Crackers
Death in Distribution
A Killing in the Family
A Theatrical Murder
Trial by Fire
Peril in Palmanova
The Squire's Lodge Murders
Murder at the Treasure Hunt
A Cornish Killing

Fantastic Books
Great Authors

darkstroke is
an imprint of
Crooked Cat Books

- Gripping Thrillers
- Cosy Mysteries
- Romantic Chick-Lit
- Fascinating Historicals
- Exciting Fantasy
- Young Adult and Children's Adventures
- Non-Fiction

Discover us online
www.darkstroke.com

Find us on instagram:
www.instagram.com/darkstrokebooks

Printed in Great Britain
by Amazon